THE NIGHT SEARCHERS

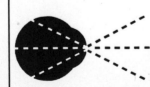

This Large Print Book carries the
Seal of Approval of N.A.V.H.

THE NIGHT SEARCHERS

MARCIA MULLER

THORNDIKE PRESS

A part of Gale, Cengage Learning

GALE
CENGAGE Learning·

Farmington Hills, Mich • San Francisco • New York • Waterville, Maine
Meriden, Conn • Mason, Ohio • Chicago

LIBRARY OF CONGRESS CATALOGING-IN-PUBLICATION DATA

Muller, Marcia.
 The night searchers / Marcia Muller. — Large print edition.
  pages cm. — (A Sharon McCone mystery) (Thorndike Press large print mystery)
 ISBN 978-1-4104-6753-9 (hardcover) — ISBN 1-4104-6753-8 (hardcover)
 1. McCone, Sharon (Fictitious character)—Fiction. 2. Women detectives—California—Fiction. 3. California—Fiction. 4. Large type books.
 I. Title.
 PS3563.U397N54 2014b
 13'.54—dc23   2014016062

Published in 2014 by arrangement with Grand Central Publishing, a division of Hachette Book Group, Inc.

Printed in the United States of America
1 2 3 4 5 6 7 18 17 16 15 14

For Karen and Ken Turner
Tobey too!

Thanks, as always, to Bill Pronzini — for his ideas, criticism, and hand-holding.

And to my editor, Dianne Choie, whose insight and eye for detail are invaluable.

Starting over when you've pretty much lost everything dear to you in a material sense is one of the most difficult things a human being can do.

In my case, I'd lost my home on Church Street where I'd lived for over two decades and all that was in it to fire. Also my car and almost my life.

On the other hand, nobody had died, my neighbors' houses hadn't been damaged, and even my cats had survived unscathed. For those blessings, I'd thanked God.

As a long-ago-lapsed Catholic, I don't thank God frequently or easily.

The list of things — some irreplaceable and some not — included photographs and mementoes; my diplomas from high school and UC–Berkeley. My favorite books, records, tapes, and DVDs. My collection — no, proliferation — of unusual paperweights, now cracked or shattered. My other collection of sequined baseball caps — red, gold, black with silver stars. The bookends — two rabbits purchased years ago at great cost from Gump's by Hy — that supported my *Webster's Unabridged Dictionary.* The dictionary itself; I seldom used it any more, the Internet being quicker and easier, but sometimes I browsed through it, picking up esoteric etymology.

What is the esoteric etymology for devastation?

Hy and I are more fortunate than most disaster victims: we own two other homes: the ranch he inherited from his stepfather in the high desert country of Mono County and Touchstone, our getaway place — which a grateful client sold me for a dollar — on the Mendocino Coast. But both were inconvenient to our businesses in San Francisco. Hy's firm, RI, had a hospitality suite for clients that was currently vacant, so we moved in there. But we had nothing except the simple amenities RI provided.

Insurance money was coming, so we shopped for a new house. The very first day of our quest we found one on Avila Street in the Bay-side Marina district: Spanish mission style, with whitewashed stucco walls and a red-tiled roof. Spacious courtyard with a hot tub and — of all things — a garden gnome. Four bedrooms, one for us, two for at-home

10

offices, one for guests.

I've always loved the Marina: on foggy days you can hear the horns bellowing out beyond the Gate, and when the sun breaks through, it seems to touch the district first. Hy was crazy about the house — he claimed it was the garden gnome that hooked him — so we put in an offer the next day.

Somebody outbid us. Gloom abounded in the RI hospitality suite, which we now thought too small and confining.

We continued looking: on Potrero Hill and Bernal Heights, where the sun shines most of the time; in Cole Valley, with its handsome — although prim — Edwardian homes; in the Haight and Cow Hollow and Pacific Heights. Nothing matched up to the "garden gnome house," as we'd taken to calling it.

And then came the message from the real estate agent: the high bidder's deal on the Avila Street house had fallen through; did we still want it? We signed the contract that evening.

We were on our way: starting over.

Now we got into consumerism in a big, bad way. Sofas for the living room: dark, buttery leather, to be grouped around the kiva fireplace; coffee and end tables, sturdy, so they could take abuse. We indulged ourselves and bought a Sleep Number bed (my side #35,

Hy's #55); a kitchen island with a wood-block top; a full set of All-Clad cookware. Dishes and flatware and linens and towels. By the time we were ready to move in, when all of the above were waiting in the terra-cotta-tiled entryway to be released from their cardboard cartons, we both felt nauseated from acquiring. The house, which we'd loved so much, felt alien. Even the garden gnome looked bleak.

Our cats, Alex and Jessie, fared better than we did: after snooping around the house and sniffing every object, they fell into their usual patterns, mainly mowling for food and sleeping on our bed.

We decided to burrow in like them, and it worked.

TUESDAY, MARCH 6

1:20 p.m.

The eyes of the prospective client who sat across my desk were pale blue, with pupils whose depth seemed to have no end. Around each iris was a circle of darker blue, a stark contrast to the whites. The woman's gaze skipped about my office — from the wall hangings to the carpeting to the bookcases and file cabinets — but never once touched on me. I finally drew her attention by tapping my pencil on her file.

The eyes fixed on mine. "I *did* see it. Even if the police and *he* don't believe me." She jerked her pointed chin at the man who stood behind her chair, hands on her shoulders.

"Cammie —" he began.

"Camilla! How many times have I told you my name's Camilla?"

"Camilla." He closed his eyes and the lines around his mouth whitened.

She shrugged his hands off and looked back at me. "Why is it so difficult to go back to your full name after a lifetime of nicknames? Why is it people like *him* can't remember?"

Frankly, I was on the husband's side.

Camilla and Jay Givens. Attractive young owners of a condo on Russian Hill, one of the city's classier districts. Recommended to me by Glenn Solomon, my friend and an esteemed criminal defense attorney.

At first I'd taken Jay Givens also to be an attorney: his Gucci loafers, crisp blue shirt, and tailored chinos spoke of lawyers' casual dress. But it turned out he was CEO of one of the city's medium-size CPA firms. Wife Camilla — short blond ponytail that reminded me of a whisk broom, tank top, long flowing skirt, hand-tooled leather cowboy boots — worked at, as she said, "little things." What little things? I'd asked. Well, she'd been an interviewer for a small radio station in Berkeley, until they'd gone broke. And she'd written a column for an ecology-oriented magazine there. Two columns, actually, before that firm had also failed. And then there were her Hawaiian shirt company and her silk-screened scarf company . . .

Camilla's specialty appeared to be killing

16

off endangered companies or those of her own devising. I had no doubt that she was talented, articulate, and motivated. But none of her ventures had worked out, and I could understand the reason: she was an emotional defective.

Not a very orthodox medical diagnosis, but I have a certifiable half brother who spends his life in and out of institutions. There's a feel to the condition, almost a smell to it, and both emanated from her now. I glanced at her husband; it was his diagnosis too.

"Okay," I said, "let's go over the facts once more. Pretend we're just starting out. You were walking in your neighborhood —"

"Russian Hill."

"At around seven o'clock last Wednesday night —"

"Seven ten."

"And you were passing a vacant lot on Saturn Street where the basement for a new apartment building has been excavated. Then you saw —"

"People down there."

"Homeless people?"

"No. They had an expensive umbrella, like the marketplace ones you see on restaurant patios. And an outdoor fireplace, probably bought from Williams-Sonoma. There was a roaring fire in it, and I think they were about to sacrifice an infant."

I glanced at Jay Givens. He winced and again placed his hands on his wife's shoulders.

"Did you see this infant?" I asked.

"No, but I heard her cry."

"How do you know it was a girl?"

"I just know, that's all."

"Why do you think they were going to sacrifice her?"

"Well, that's what they do, isn't it? Those kind of people?"

When I'd questioned the woman before about what "those kind of people" were like, the rambling answer she'd given me had made no sense. This one wouldn't either. Fortunately I was taping our conversation; maybe I could interpret it better when I went over it.

I ran the tip of my tongue over my lips, made a nonsense symbol on my legal pad, and asked, "What kind of people?"

She was leaning forward, trying to read what I'd written on the pad; I shielded it from her sight. "Those people . . . ?" I prompted.

"Devil worshippers."

Jay Givens let go an audible sigh, but his

wife was so into her story she didn't hear him.

"They do these things to appease Satan, but they don't want to do them in their homes because the fire and burning flesh would stink them up. They're all affluent like Jay and me — that's how they got to be."

This was a fantasy she hadn't voiced before. "They made pacts with the devil?"

Camilla Givens nodded solemnly.

"You mentioned that the people were affluent like you and your husband. Neither of you made a pact with the devil, did you?"

Indignant look. "Of course not! Jay's very smart, and I'm very creative. We made our own success. Those people are sly but stupid and need help."

Oh, lord! Secret meetings in an excavated basement — with marketplace umbrellas and Williams-Sonoma outdoor stoves. Barbecued babies. Maybe a goat or two? Hoods . . . ?

I asked, "Were they wearing hoods?"

"Oh, yes, hoods. But the people weren't the Klan. The Klan's hoods are pointy, but those people's were round, to fit their heads. But long, down to their elbows."

At this point Jay Givens turned around and mimed banging his head against the wall. His little act annoyed me. Why had he brought his wife here with her ridiculous tale, rather than to a psychiatrist? Why had Glenn Solomon referred them to me?

Camilla Givens was watching me eagerly.

I said, "Let me do a little exploration, and tomorrow we'll talk some more."

Neither of them asked what the exploration would be, nor what it would cost. That was okay; the sum total of it would be a conversation with Glenn.

2:55 p.m.

"Glenn, why on earth did you send the Givens couple to me?"

We were seated in a booth at Temple Bar on Lime Alley near the Federal Building where he had been appealing a case. Besides being a lawyers' and politicians' hangout, the bar was a throwback to the gaslight days, with leather banquettes, red-flocked wallpaper, chandeliers hung with crystal teardrops and turned low. The floor was covered with ancient Oriental carpets, and the ceiling with decorative tin panels. There was a residue of long-ago cigar smoke that nothing short of tearing down the building would eradicate.

Glenn sipped his martini and said, "You thought the wife was insane, right?"

"Isn't she?"

"Maybe. When they first came to my office to discuss this . . . problem they've been having, she seemed strange enough to be scary."

I sipped my wine, said, "Glenn, today you were arguing an appeal for a client who's been convicted of killing seven people. *He's* not scary?"

"There's a difference. He was in manacles and a San Quentin jumpsuit, with guards standing by. Besides," he added, "he's innocent."

"Come on. You don't really believe that. They're *all* innocent — according to them."

"Some are, some aren't. But I give them as good a defense as I can because, my friend, they are all equal under the law — including the defendants in the pro bono cases I take on for zip dollars." He made a gesture of cash flowing through his fingers. "Those clients are at greater risk because they're poor, badly educated, ethnic, and can't speak out for themselves. I speak for them."

"And you also soak your rich clients."

He laughed. "Hell, why not? They're glad to pay because they're usually so goddamn guilty!"

I laughed too. "Let's get back to the Givenses. Anything you can tell me about them that Mick can't get off the Internet?" Mick Savage, my nephew, had transformed the agency with his search skills, and now he and another operative, Derek Ford, were making yet more strides in the area of investigative work. Their search engine, SavageFor, had sold to the giant — and well-named — Omnivore, and a more state-of-the-art version, 4S, would go public in months.

Glenn looked thoughtful. "Going to consult the old memory bank for a couple of minutes."

As he held his "consultation" I looked around the bar. An assistant district attorney with whom I'd had dealings was at one end, attempting to entrance a young woman with beautiful long dark hair. (He wouldn't score.) At the other end, an aide to the current mayor had his head together with a well-known freelance publicist. (The city needed the publicist; the mayor was, as usual, in trouble.) A minor real-estate tycoon held an intense conversation with a developer. (It was a false show, probably put on for someone else present in the crowd; in reality, they hated each other.)

Glenn said, "My friend, are you still in there?"

"What? Oh, I'm just watching the future

of the city evolve around me."

He gave the other patrons a dark look. "This crowd gets its paws on real power, and they'll turn the city to shit."

"Why do you come here, then?"

"Know thine enemy."

It was getting late, and I had other things to finish up, so I said, "About the Givenses?"

"Right." He ran a hand over his thick white hair. "I don't know either of the Givenses very well, but Jay's father Roy was a close friend for years. He died on the golf course at Pebble Beach last August. That's why I have good reason to stay away from those death traps." Portly Glenn was openly averse to exercise in any form. "Anyway, I suppose they felt more comfortable with a known quantity like me when Camilla started having her . . . little problems."

"Is there something about these 'little problems' that would indicate Camilla needs a criminal lawyer? Or a detective, rather than a good psychiatrist?"

"Because when they brought me Camilla's extremely unbelievable tale, I sensed something."

"What?"

"Hard to put into words. In my profession, as in yours, we rely on intuition and

23

our imperfect knowledge of the human psyche. Something was, in cop jargon, hinky."

"With the husband or the wife?"

"Both."

"How?"

"He acted condescending — indulge the little screwball, you know. She was frightened — of him or of these episodes, I can't say."

"Episodes? Plural?"

"They didn't tell you about the others?"

"No."

Glenn looked at his watch. "I have to meet a client on the Peninsula in an hour, so that gives us time to go back to my office and access my file on the Givenses. You free?"

"For now."

3:21 p.m.

While Glenn searched for the Givens file, with the great mumbling and grumbling of a person who delegates all but the most simple computer tasks to his minions, I enjoyed the panoramic view from his office in Four Embarcadero Center.

I grew up in San Diego, but while I was a student at UC–Berkeley the Bay Area claimed me as one of its own. The great expanses of waterways and bridges crossing

24

them; the towering hills that were either pine-forested, peopled, or severely barren; the lights of the houses twinkling through the trees at night; the variety of architectural styles; the blending of past and future that permeates today's lifestyle — all of them touched my heart as no other place ever had. I'd never looked back.

Now traffic was slowing up on the north-bound lanes of the Golden Gate Bridge — early for a Monday. An excursion boat chugged along steadily; I could imagine the voice of the guide bellowing through a microphone at the captive audience of tourists. Media choppers buzzed low, monitoring the commute; a jet out of SFO left contrails in the blue sky. A beautiful, picture-perfect day.

Of course, it was March, and that meant picture-perfect wouldn't stay around for long. Although our weather has strayed from its usual patterns with the encroachment of global warming, January through March is typically our rainy season. If you're here then, you'd better have an umbrella and hat close at hand.

"Ah shit!" Glenn threw up his hands in resignation. "I can't find it. I've had so many temps in, and I swear each has a different techno-language."

"Where's Ms. Hamlin?" I asked. She'd been Glenn's secretary for several years.

"Where d'you think? She's gone East — to law school at Michigan."

Secretaries were always leaving Glenn for law school; his excellent tutelage gave them too much enthusiasm to resist the call of higher education. It was to his credit that he supplied them with glowing recommendations.

"What about a paper file?" I asked.

"The temps have different alphabets as well."

"You're going to be late for your meeting. If you trust me, I'll stay and try to access the file."

"If I trust you? Why wouldn't I?"

"This computer contains a treasure trove of confidential information."

"Which I know you have no intention of accessing." His eyes twinkled as he shrugged into his suit coat. "Besides," he added, "I didn't give you my password, did I? Just shut her down when you leave. I'll alert building security that you're working up here."

6:58 p.m.

My eyes felt as if there were sand under their lids, and my head throbbed dully when

I descended to the garage at Four Embarcadero, my arms full of printed pages. For a couple of hours I'd tried to digest what I found on Glenn's computer, but I was reading too fast and taking too few notes, so in the end I'd printed out the whole file. Glenn's printer didn't like me — or maybe I was just incompetent — and it kept jamming pages. My hands were covered with ink stains from trying to free them, and what little patience I had was razor-thin. I tossed the pages on the passenger seat of my car, where they promptly slipped onto the floor. I sighed and headed back to my offices in the RI building on New Montgomery.

I had mixed feelings about the building and the new offices. The offices were elegant — very, very elegant. Deeply piled carpets; attractive and functional contemporary furnishings; posters from special events at the city's museums brightening the pale-gray walls. My own space was a dream: it had an expansive view from the Golden Gate to the East Bay hills, a huge cherry-wood desk and matching bookcases and file cabinets; a full-length sofa so I wouldn't have to lie on the floor during my "quiet times" (anything from a full-blown snit to deep slumber). My age-old armchair, originally from a closet under the stairs at All Souls Legal Cooperative, but now restored in leather, and its newish matching hassock were positioned by the windows under a healthy potted schefflera plant named Mr. T., after Ted Smalley, my office manager. The Grand Poobah, as he prefers to call himself, had decorated the suite singlehandedly.

That was the good part. The bad part: I wasn't used to such an upscale environment. For years my agency had had offices in Pier 24 1/2, which was now in the process of being demolished, and I'd loved it there, drafty and cold and echoing as it was.

Before that I'd had first the closet and then an upstairs room at All Souls' big Victorian in Bernal Heights, in the southeastern section of the city. The poverty law firm, headed by my best male friend, Hank Zahn, had subsisted in the big broken-down house, with some employees living in and others — mercifully, including me — living out. But most of the friendships forged there had carried on to this day, and when the co-op folded, I'd managed to bring Ted along to my new agency.

Maybe I was just used to downscale, but many times when I came through the door of the high-security RI building — express line, where all the guards knew me — I felt as if I were sneaking in under false pretenses. The offices seemed to demand that I be superior to who I really was: dress better, use more artfully applied makeup, and for Christ's sake get those nails done!

All this paranoia induced by a *building*! One owned by my husband and, by extension of California's community property law, by me.

There were message slips on my desk: my mothers (I have two — Ma, my adoptive parent in San Diego, and Saskia, my birth mother in Boise) had both called. My best friend Rae Kelleher had told Ted she was bored; her husband, country music star Ricky Savage, was in L.A. dealing with some problem at his record company. Hank Zahn wanted to have lunch soon. No business calls; I felt lucky to have a few clients in this economy, when most firms and individuals didn't have the ready cash for outside help.

I logged on to my computer, saw Mick had e-mailed me the results of some searches I'd asked him to run while I was at Glenn's office. I pulled them up and set my own printer to work. Fortunately *it* liked me. After a while I drifted over to my old armchair, closed my eyes under the spreading branches of Mr. T., and let the facts of the Givens case percolate randomly through my mind.

In particular, the other "episodes."

After going over them, I had ranked each as genuine, possible, doubtful, or impossible.

Three months ago, almost to the day, Camilla had seen a clown driving on the freeway. Possible: Many clowns, such as Ronald McDonalds, drove to work fully dressed in costume.

Two weeks later she saw a figure jump from the Golden Gate Bridge. Possible. Every year a few suicides go unnoticed by both persons crossing and the Bridge Authority.

The next month her tale was of a white horse galloping down the twisty part of Lombard Street just before dusk. Doubtful. None of the residents of that fabled block had seen it or heard anything resembling hoofbeats.

Three weeks later a homeless man urinated in a trash can on Jones Street and then set it on fire. Camilla had put the fire out with her bare hands. Yes, such a thing had happened, but a neighbor had put out the blaze with an extinguisher and made a report to the fire department. In addition, Camilla and Jay had been at their getaway place near Lake Tahoe on the date in question. Impossible.

And so it went, the incidents coming closer together and edging more and more toward the doubtful/impossible end of the scale, until this recent infant-sacrifice tale — which, of course, I had labeled impossible.

In the morning I'd call Jay Givens and tell him he should contact a psychiatrist. But something about such a cold dismissal bothered me. In spite of my better judgment, I kept poring over Glenn's files.

9:55 p.m.

My God, I'd lost track of the time! Fallen asleep, actually.

Now I felt great. Rested and ready to . . . what?

Call Hy, and tell him I'd be home shortly.

Something in me balked at that. At home, the conversation would be about what colors to paint the rooms, and the plumber's estimate, while we both skirted around the how-was-your-day topic, something we weren't allowed to talk about because of the security regulations of both our firms. Then it would turn to Hy's hopes to merge our companies so we could become a partnership in every meaning of the word. And I

31

didn't want to go there. Not yet.

My cell rang, startling me.

"Hey, McCone," Hy said, "I'm glad I caught you. I'll be away for a while, don't know how long yet. There's been a situation, and a high-level hostage negotiation's going down. I'll keep in touch."

And here RI company policy kicked in. "Okay," I said. "Love you."

"You too."

I wondered where he was off to. A high-level hostage negotiation? That could be anywhere in the world. Hy was known as the best negotiator in his field, but some of those types of tricky confrontations ended in bloodshed.

Well, we were both leading the lives we'd chosen, weren't we?

To take my mind off grim thoughts, I turned my attention back to Mick's research. The vacant lot on the corner of Saturn and Leavenworth Streets on Russian Hill had been owned for the past two years by the Kenyon brothers, Dick and Chad. They'd begun to dig the basement immediately, but then construction was halted.

I knew of the Kenyon brothers. They were people who bought things: real estate, both residential and commercial; land, as far away as Montana; commodities futures;

small, profitable businesses; hotels, motels, and restaurants; gold, silver, and diamonds; racehorses. None of these had any particular meaning for them or remained in their possession very long; their objective was to turn them quickly for a profit. So far as I'd heard, the only thing the brothers cared about was money — and over the past twenty years they'd amassed hundreds of millions.

So why dig a basement for the apartment building they'd announced they would be constructing and then abandon the project for a year and a half? Obviously they weren't interested in the property any more, so why not sell it?

Oh, hell. Did I really care at this hour? It was close to midnight, and I was tired.

As I was leaving my office, a fact from the files surfaced, and I had to go back and confirm it.

Right: GW&G Associates, Jay Givens's CPA firm, was the accountant of record for the Kenyon brothers. Obviously Givens had known his clients owned the lot where his wife claimed she had observed a bizarre spectacle. Why hadn't he mentioned it?

■ ■ ■ ■

WEDNESDAY, MARCH 7

■ ■ ■ ■

12:44 a.m.

Russian Hill was more or less on my way home, so I decided to take a look at the vacant lot.

No one was on the sidewalks of Leavenworth Street when I drove up to where it intersected with Saturn. The neighborhood was mostly commercial, and the occasional corner stores and small restaurants were closed. Muted light shone behind window coverings in the upper stories of a few of the buildings, and I could hear the mumblings of TV sets, but otherwise all was still. I drove by the chain link fence enclosing the property but couldn't make out anything in the darkness, so I found a parking place a block away and walked back there.

The lot was small by commercial standards — maybe twenty-five by forty feet. It was on a corner, surrounded on two sides by windowless walls of commercial buildings; catercorner was a residential hotel that appeared to be closed; opposite it sat a boarded-up structure.

This was another example of the changing face of the city: when I'd first moved here, Polk Street had been a haven for gays, a bustling, hustling thoroughfare peopled by zany shoppers and equally zany shopkeepers. Now, at least at this end, near the Civic Center, it was grim and grimy and silent; a few blocks down, music and other assorted sounds rose from the nightclubs that dominated there. Tomorrow the SFPD would have logged dozens of calls from those living on the hill above, complaining about the racket.

The fence surrounding the vacant lot sagged and there were metal signs affixed to it at intervals:

NO ADMITTANCE

SECURITY PROVIDED BY GLASKIRK, INC.

TRESPASSERS WILL BE PROSECUTED

I smiled. Glaskirk had been one of the worst security companies in the Bay Area. In fact, it had been so inept that I'd turned down a job there when I was a desperate, no-skills sociology grad from UC–Berkeley. It had been out of business for nine years now. These were old signs, judging from the amount of rust on them.

I was approaching carefully about thirty yards from the fence, hidden by the shadow of an overhang on the dark adjacent building, when a slight motion stopped me. A figure was slipping through a gap next to one of the fence poles. Something about the way it moved was familiar —

Hy.

I stifled a gasp by clamping my hand to my lips. Anger sparked and spread through me. How I hated to be lied to! Especially by someone I trusted more than —

I hurried back to my car. From the trunk I took a pair of old athletic shoes and a multi-pocketed down vest — a wardrobe I kept there for emergencies. I put them on and armed myself with a powerful flashlight equipped with a special lens cap that made its beam inconspicuous to anyone except the searcher. In the vest pockets I had a small infrared camera, a highly sensitive tape recorder, and a Swiss Army knife. There was yet another pocket meant to hold a gun, but I'd stuffed it with a couple of pairs of gloves instead. Last year I'd investigated a complicated case involving the gun control issue, and after it was over, I'd decided that firepower would no longer play a part in my life — at least for now.

When I got back to the fence I couldn't spot Hy. I approached the gap where he'd entered. Peered through and down. No light or other motion below. What to do now? Certainly not bellow his name down there to get his attention.

If I followed, I would be trespassing — an offense that, if I was caught, could prompt the state board to hold a hearing and lift my license, possibly destroying my livelihood and credibility. Could a good lawyer prove just cause for such an act? In the back of my mind I heard Glenn Solomon's voice saying, "Don't do it."

I've never taken advice — however wise — well.

I slipped through the open space in the fence, then paused to listen and stare downward into the darkness.

No sounds. And nothing to see except shapes that turned out to be slabs of broken concrete. The ground was sandy, with outcroppings of hard rock, and little trails of soil trickled down after me as I descended. Then I tripped on something and skidded the rest of the way.

At the bottom of the excavated area, I

pushed up and switched on my flash. It revealed a scene similar to those in post-apocalyptic sci-fi movies. Rubble: earth and concrete and stone. Piles of dirt poised on the brink of toppling. Trash that people had dumped: beer cans and pop bottles; torn newspapers and magazines; an ancient transistor radio; broken glass and flowerpots and crockery; Styrofoam cups and food wrappers. All the garbage that people with no regard for the planet had discarded, rather than disposing of properly.

"Ripinsky?" I whispered.

No response.

There was a cleared space in the center of all the junk, and as I approached it my flashlight showed a pile of charred wood. I went closer, studied the ground around it. Plastic jugs, food wrappers. A standard meal for homeless people — fortunate homeless people. The majority did without.

No indication of satanic infant sacrifices. No discarded hoods. Nothing but a place that beckoned to those who had lost everything — or never had it.

Hy's voice spoke in a fierce whisper behind me: "What the hell are you doing here, McCone?"

"I thought it was you. I saw you sneaking in," I said in the same fierce whisper. "So you're still in the city."

"Obviously."

"Why did you lie to me?"

"I didn't. All I said was I would be away for a while."

"What about the hostage negotiation?"

"That'll be clear to you in due time. Now what're *you* doing here?"

I shook my head. "No, I asked you first."

"You sound like this is a kids' game."

"We're neither of us kids. Answer me!"

"Sssh. Come on over behind that foundation wall. It's the best vantage point I could find."

"Vantage point for what?"

"Not now."

He guided me over the rough ground and we sat. The night was cold, and I was glad to have on my down vest. As it was, the cold of the ground penetrated my jeans and my nose already felt half frozen. Hy put his arm around me, and we leaned back against the incline.

"If we're lucky," he said, "we won't have to wait long. If anything happens, you stay put and let me handle it."

"What're we waiting for? What could happen?"

"Let it go for now, McCone. We shouldn't talk down here — too dangerous."

7:37 a.m.

We weren't lucky, because nothing happened. The time dragged on, and at some point I must've dozed off, because I jerked when Hy said, "All right, dammit, we've been here long enough. We'd better get out before we freeze to death."

"Home? And then you'll tell me what's going down?"

"Not home. Not yet."

"Why? Don't tell me there's a chance that what happened to our old house is happening to the new one." I had a mental image of the billowing smoke and all-consuming flames of the fire — a fire set by a disgruntled client of mine — that had destroyed our house on Church Street.

"No, don't worry about that."

"Well, then, where?"

"A new safe house."

RI maintained various safe houses in the cities where it had offices: out-of-the way, innocuous-looking buildings in neighborhoods where people kept to themselves and had little contact with or interest in others.

43

Inside each house, however, was a fully staffed security operation to protect at-risk clients. I'd stayed in one myself a while back, and had found the ever-watchful eyes of the guards and cameras oppressive in the extreme.

The typical client was grateful for his or her safety, but often imperious and demanding, as highly placed persons tend to be: requests for exotic food and drink in the middle of the night; demands that linens and towels be changed more than once a day; sneaky outside phone calls that were strictly taboo; the incessant need for fresh flowers, perfume, hairstyling, and massages — all of these rasped on the nerves of the caregivers, who thought that the self-styled important personages should simply feel goddamned lucky to be alive. As a result, RI had a quick turnover of personnel at all locations.

And now Hy was telling me that they had a new safe house. I couldn't wait to see it.

8:01 a.m.
It turned out to be a hot sheet motel on the Great Highway near the zoo. The carpet in the unit that Hy steered me to was threadbare, the headboard painted red and carved with hearts and the names of many loving

44

couples. There was even a mirror on the ceiling.

"My God," I said, "you *bought* this dump?"

"This dump, as you call it, is one of the safest we have in the city, and the security is fully manned from our downtown office." Hy was checking the locks on the windows.

"What kind of clients do you plan to put here? Sleazy ones? Horny ones?"

"You'd be surprised who's going to stay here — and be plenty grateful for it."

He went around a little table with two chairs, removed a device from the phone jack, and tossed it to me. Then he sat down in one of the chairs, motioned me to the other. As I sat I touched the table, quickly withdrew my hand from a sticky spot.

He grimaced. "We had to let the housekeeping staff go — not that they were big on cleanliness anyway, and our operatives aren't much better. Before we start putting clients up here, I hope to get hold of some good maintenance people."

"About the clients . . . ?"

"Let's just say they'll all be in great fear."

"Of the cockroaches or the bedbugs?"

"They'll be fast friends with all kinds of varmints before they leave."

Hy's phone rang. He answered, spoke

tersely into it. A few seconds after he broke the connection, it rang again. I could tell little from his side of the conversations. After the phone rang a third and fourth time, he punched in a forwarding number and set it down.

"The office'll buzz me if it's an important call." RI's offices around the world were staffed 24-7, and all reported hourly to the San Francisco headquarters.

"About what? What's so damned important?"

"What were you doing at that vacant lot?"

"Working a case. What were you doing there?"

"The same."

"And now we're going to sit here and discuss confidentiality till we're both out of our minds."

"The hell with confidentiality."

That surprised me. "Never thought I'd hear you say that."

"I'm sick of all these rules: need-to-know basis and so forth. I didn't make them up in the first place — Dan and Gage did. But Dan's dead, Gage is God knows where, and now I'm running the show. Confidentiality has its place, but not between you and me, especially since we seem to be working the same case."

46

The people he spoke of — Dan Kessell and Gage Renshaw — had founded Renshaw & Kessell International, the firm that evolved into RI after Kessell was murdered and Renshaw fled the country because of the collapse of one of his complicated scams.

"The cases are — ?" Hy prompted me.

"Similar, anyway. I gather you've brought me here because we can't talk at home. Is the house bugged?"

"Probably not. I just sent technicians out to go over the place to make sure. They'll also clear our offices."

"And you're absolutely sure no one can eavesdrop on us here?"

"Yes. That device I disconnected" — he gestured at the small cylinder in my hand — "connects with an RI operative twenty-four seven. It also monitors the entire safe house. Nothing happens here that doesn't communicate to RI's office if it's working."

I set the listening device down on the sticky spot. "But aren't there others, in other rooms?"

"No, this one works for the entire premises. I deliberately chose this room because it's so awful nobody would think there was anything worth finding here."

"It's awful, all right."

"McCone, I'm disappointed. I'd planned to spend our second honeymoon here."

10:04 a.m.

Hy, he told me, actually was involved in a hostage negotiation. That was why he'd gone to the vacant lot. An RI client, Van Hoffman, had vanished two nights ago on the way from his office on the thirty-fifth floor of the Transamerica Pyramid to his car on the first level of the underground parking garage. Hoffman was director of the influential Global Policy Forum, an advisor to governments and powerful individuals. He was married, had two adult children, lived in the affluent Peninsula suburb of Atherton, and was rumored to be a workaholic with few outside interests. When he failed to return home as expected, his wife, Jane, had contacted RI, with whom Global had an executive protection agreement.

Such agreements, which covered key players in various types of firms, became popular in the late 1980s when a rash of hostage-taking plagued the burgeoning bio- and high-tech industries. For a set yearly fee, a company could take out insurance on executives critical to its operations, and RI — then called Renshaw & Kessell International — would provide surveillance and train personnel in evasion techniques and defensive driving. Should a hostage situation occur, Hy would step in as negotiator.

He said, "At least Jane Hoffman understood what to do if he didn't return home at the assigned time. So many of our clients try to protect their families from insecurity and don't tell them about our services. Or the potential risks to them. They're usually the ones we lose."

It wasn't until six o'clock the night before that a message had appeared on Hy's business e-mail account:

WE HAVE YOUR CLIENT VAN HOFFMAN AND ARE READY TO NEGOTIATE. DETAILS TO FOLLOW.

It had, Hy said, been a tense wait. The person made appointments, then broke them; teased and taunted:

SEVEN FIFTEEN. UNDER THE BAY BRIDGE NEAR WHAT USED TO BE PIER 24 1/2. YOU KNOW WHERE THAT IS, DON'T YOU?

"They know about you and me," I said.

HEY, DON'T RUSH OUT THE DOOR. I'VE CHANGED MY MIND. HOW ABOUT LANDS END? NO, TOO COLD THERE FOR MY BLOOD.

GUESS WE'LL RESCHEDULE FOR NINE FIF-
TEEN. HOW ABOUT THE VACANT LOT WHERE
YOUR HOUSE BURNED DOWN?

"Yeah, he knows a lot about us," Hy said.
All the time RI's technicians had been trying to get a fix on the IP address the e-mails
were coming from. No luck — it changed
with each message.
More messages:

SPEAKING OF VACANT LOTS . . . NO, NOT YET.

MIDNIGHT? THE WITCHING HOUR? THAT
WOULD BE APPROPRIATE.

THIS GUY, YOUR CLIENT, VAN HOFFMAN, HE
HOLDS VALUABLE SECRETS. LET'S SEE IF
HE'LL GIVE THEM UP.

A half hour later:

NOPE. HE'S A TOUGH ONE. WE'LL MAKE ONE
MORE TRY.

Another half hour:

HE'S EITHER VERY STRONG OR VERY STUPID.
  HOW COME THE MEDIA HAVEN'T GOTTEN
HOLD OF THIS? IT'S A NATIONAL SECURITY
RISK.

50

Fifteen minutes later:

THERE'S A VACANT LOT AT LEAVENWORTH
AND SATURN STREETS. COME THERE AT ONE
A.M.

BRING $45,000 IN SMALL BILLS TO RANSOM
YOUR CLIENT, OR WE WILL USE EXTREME
METHODS TO MAKE HIM GIVE UP HIS SE-
CRETS.

"The person e-mailing you," I said,
"must've been piggybacking off other people's accounts. All you need to do for that is
wait outside some building with a laptop till
you pick up a signal."

"That's how I've got it figured. The odd
thing is," he added, "the ransom demand. I
reported it to Mrs. Hoffman, and she said it
was exactly the amount they have in their
savings account."

"People with sophisticated skills can
always hack into bank accounts. Did you
bring the money?"

"No. We don't pay off hostage takers;
Hoffman knew that when his firm signed
the contract with us."

"How does Mrs. Hoffman feel about
that?"

"Hard to tell. She's a very remote
woman."

"Just how important to national security are the issues Hoffman deals with, d'you suppose?"

"I don't know, not yet. But I've got operatives working on it, both here and in D.C. It's odd, because Hoffman seemed an unlikely candidate to be snatched. The Global Policy Forum is about to lose its government funding and be dissolved."

"Why?"

"It's rumored that they're ineffectual, don't have access to important information, and have pissed off a number of influential politicians."

"Politicians!" I snorted. "So why would they bother with Hoffman?"

"Good question."

"Maybe someone in his family has an idea. Do you know any of them?"

"Just as names in a file. We were hired by his employer, not them."

"Send me their contact information."

"Why?"

"Because there's one big connection between your case and mine — that vacant lot."

"So what *is* your case?"

I told him in detail.

Hy said, "What if Hoffman and the Givenses are linked in some way?"

"You think? Jay Givens is a CPA with a good firm."

"And according to you, Camilla's crazy."

"Maybe she's not crazy after all. Maybe she's a good actress, working from a script. When I meet with her again, I'll have a better idea."

"How?"

"By listening to what she says — and listening to her silences."

Listen to the silence.

The phrase had come back to me from years before, when I'd been searching for the identities of my birth parents. There had been a lot of silences during my life, particularly when I was growing up, and it had taken the revelation that I was adopted to interpret them as substitutes for lies. Since then I've been alert for those telltale lapses, and recognizing them for what they are serves me well in my investigations.

11:02 a.m.

Our house on Avila Street was still being swept by RI's technicians, so after I left Hy at Cockroach Haven, as I'd named the new safe house, I grabbed a super-large cup of coffee at Big Bad Bubba's on Geary and went back to the office.

I felt grubby and tired, but I called Camilla Givens to make an appointment to see her alone at eight that evening, then showered in the agency's large, fully equipped bathroom and took a nap on my sofa. I keep a few changes of clothes in the armoire in my office; I selected the outfit best suited for a business meeting, went through the papers that had accumulated in my in box — including another message from Ma, whose persistence is legendary — and checked my e-mail. Nothing from Mick.

My nephew, after a couple of harrowing experiences, professed not to want to do fieldwork any more, but every now and then he came up with an intriguing lead and went off on the hunt. The agency has a rule that operatives check in twice daily, but so far it had failed to penetrate his stubborn skull. Of course, there could be a simple explanation for his silence: he and his woman friend Alison were moving from a condo in one of the high-rises that — increasingly — overshadow our city's formerly light-filled downtown streets, to the more pleasant clime of Potrero Hill. They'd probably gotten caught up in packing and transporting. They'd hated high-rise living and had also gone through a dicey time lately — a pregnancy scare and Alison's so-far-undiagnosed inherited health issue. I was happy to see them settling into a life-style that suited them both.

3:18 p.m.

RI's technicians were finally done sweeping and had found no bugs at our house or offices. After finishing up some routine work and giving operatives Julia Rafael, Craig Morland, Adah Joslyn, and Patrick Neilan a heads-up that I might be needing them for surveillances over the next few days, I picked up the printout from Mick and took it home to read in quiet.

Hy and I had only been living in the new house on Avila Street for a couple of weeks, and every time I pushed the button on the garage door opener and drove inside, I felt a proud rush of ownership. I'd always loved the area, and we were fitting right in. Adah and Craig lived in an apartment only two blocks away, and we'd already begun to get to know our neighbors. Initially they'd been leery of us: they knew us by reputation and it was only after being reassured by Hy that it was extremely unlikely we'd be shot, fire-bombed, or murdered in our bed that they had become friendly and begun issuing dinner invitations.

I wasn't convinced that we were as immune to violence as Hy claimed, but my husband is excellent at persuading people to look at things in a positive way. He persuades everybody except me. And himself.

I loved everything about the house: the terra-cotta and hardwood floors; the hand-painted tiles in the kitchen and the bathrooms; the dark wooden beams; the archways that led from room to room. The gracefully curving staircase had an intricate black iron railing; the kitchen had been updated, but not in a way that clashed with the overall décor, and the same was true of the Jacuzzi tubs and other conveniences in the bathrooms. And then there was the hot tub and the garden gnome. Adolphus, we called him, in homage to Hy's only living relative, Uncle Al.

Normally I hate garden statuary, but Adolphus had won my heart. He was fat and jolly-looking, but not the least bit garish. And damned if he didn't resemble Hy's uncle, a rancher who lived in eastern Oregon. I planned to deck the gnome out in a red-and-green scarf and cap at Christmas, when Uncle Al was scheduled to visit.

Messages on the machine: Ma again. There would be an exhibit including two of her oil paintings at the local YWCA next month; she hoped Hy and I could make it.

My adoptive mother (who raised me) is an amazing woman. Years ago she divorced my father — who scarcely seemed to notice her absence — and remarried. When her new husband died a couple of years ago, we kids worried about her because she seemed lost for a time. Then she took an art class at the community college, and her true talents were revealed. Ma had always excelled at things — gardening, cooking, sewing — but as a painter she was something else.

Saskia Blackhawk, who put me up for adoption when I was born, is also incredible. An attorney who has argued cases for the rights of American Indians before the Supreme Court (and won), she's a high-powered, driven individual who's nevertheless able to kick back and enjoy life with the pleasure of a child. She, my half sister Robin (a law student at Berkeley), and I have enjoyed many memorable women's weekends at the coast and points east.

And then there's my birth father, Elwood Farmer. He's an artist who made a name for himself in New York many years ago, but returned to marry a Blackfoot woman and live on their reservation near Great Falls, Montana. Elwood isn't much on phone chats, but occasionally he leaves a cryptic message on my voice mail — usually at times when he thinks I won't be answering. The last one had said, "Daughter, I had a dream last night. Creatures are snapping at your heels."

Story of my life, Elwood, Daddy, whatever you want me to call you.

Neither call from the mothers required an answer just this minute, so I went to the kitchen, where Alex and Jessie began chattering for their supper. I fed them some of the evil-smelling stuff they so love, then got myself a glass of wine and took it to the living room, slipping off my shoes as I went. I've never had a decent relationship with a pair of shoes — probably never will.

The Givenses, Mick's report said, had something of an odd background. Jay was the son of Roy Givens, Glenn Solomon's classmate at Stanford, but Roy had left the family when the boy was only three. Wife Julie had divorced him and remarried quickly, to a man named Paul Sonnen; together they had set out to raise Jay, but Roy Givens returned five years later and claimed his son. Paul Sonnen was seriously ill at the time, and the couple had no funds for a custody battle, so, regretfully, they let Jay go.

With his father, Jay Givens lived a nomadic life, without ever ranging far from the Bay Area. Marginal neighborhood to marginal neighborhood. Trailer park to trailer park, each shabbier than the one before. Roy Givens drank and gambled; he taught young Jay many confidence games, and the boy was adept at them. But then, when he was thirteen, Roy Givens died of a heart attack and Jay was sent back to the Sonnens.

Overnight, everything changed: Jay had a real family; he went to school and studied hard. He was quick with figures, and in college entered a fast-track CPA program, and graduated with honors. Met Camilla Hope while he was working for a Big Eight firm in Southern California and married her three months later. Landed a plum job with an excellent accounting firm when he returned to San Francisco and climbed the ladder rapidly, soon becoming a full partner. Even though both Sonnens died a couple of years later, life had been good, until now — when Camilla appeared to have gone at least a little crazy.

Mick had done background on Camilla too: born, Orlando, Florida; BA in English literature from Florida State University; both parents deceased when she was in college; moved to Tustin, California, where she taught English at a local high school. Met Jay Givens through friends at a party. There was a list of the "little things" she'd occupied her time with since they'd moved to San Francisco, but she hadn't done anything in over a year.

Mick had appended a note saying I'd have more detailed information shortly.

My phone rang. Mick. Think of the devil . . .

"One interesting new piece of information about Jay Givens," he announced. "He has a strange hobby, according to a couple of Google sites: Urban Treasure Hunting, an Internet game. The concept is that a group of people — not necessarily known to each other — get together and donate an object of value — monetary or sentimental — to a pool. Every week or so, they nominate one member as the Hider. He or she secretes away one of the objects in an undisclosed location and then provides the others with clues as to where to start, always after dark. After that, they follow the clues. Whoever discovers the item gets to claim it."

I'd been on treasure hunts as a kid, where you'd hide something fairly worthless — such as a bag of clothespins or your brother's cast-off tennies — and leave a chain of clues leading to its whereabouts. The one who found it got a prize — usually a soft drink or a nip from somebody's parents' liquor cabinet if they were out of town. Later we graduated to joints. But something valuable to us? No way.

Well, this was an adult game; the stakes were higher. But why on earth would any reasonable adult want to play it? Strictly for the prizes? Not if the players were already well-off individuals like Jay Givens.

Okay, then, the group members were not reasonable people. The element of adventure attracted them, I supposed. Being out in the dark, searching unknown territory. Maybe taking risks of one kind or another.

Fear? That too. Adrenaline-pounding excitement. Unknowns. A return to the primal urges of the hunter. Something along the lines of why I'd been attracted to my job. Danger, I know all too well, can be highly addictive . . .

My thoughts returned to that vacant lot. Was there a connection between it and this Urban Treasure Hunting game? Or to the Hoffman kidnapping?

"You still there, Shar?"

"Yeah. Sorry. Who's that psychologist friend of Alison's — the one who teaches at SF State?"

"Terry Baldwin."

"D'you think she'd be willing to answer a few questions for me?"

"I'm sure she would. Let me give her a call, and she'll get back to you when it's convenient."

Five minutes later I was talking with Baldwin, a husky-voiced woman with faint strains of a Southern accent.

"Groups as you describe," she told me, "aren't uncommon. They provide the individual with something that's lacking in his or her life. Suppose a person who is really adventurous is stuck in a dull job and has no money to go skydiving or hang gliding or whatever turns him on. Sneaking around the city looking for treasure can alleviate some of that dead-end feeling."

"You said 'him.' Are most of the people male?"

"I would say it's about seventy-thirty percent in favor of men, but women have those needs too." She chuckled. "As you should know, Ms. McCone."

"But I don't seek danger; it comes to me."

"You sought out your profession, didn't you?"

"You've got me there."

"Of course, I don't suppose any of your fellow professionals engage in such behavior when they get together."

62

"No. Mostly we just drink and complain about getting stiffed on our fees."

She laughed. "Exactly as at every gathering of psychologists." Then her tone grew more serious. "I don't think you should underestimate the dangers presented by this . . . well, I hate to use the term *cult,* but essentially that's what they are. Mixtures of various types of personalities: some dominant, some weak; some worldly, some naïve; some control freaks, some victims."

"We've all seen the damage those combinations can do: the Manson Family, the People's Temple, the Mormon separatists."

"Yes, and if some factor disturbs the mix, tips the scales, it can lead to serious trouble. If I were you, Ms. McCone, I'd be very careful in your dealings with this group."

8:01 p.m.

I was surprised when Jay answered my ring at the Givenses' Russian Hill condo, because when I'd called to make the appointment with Camilla, I'd requested it just be the two of us. In jeans and a 49ers T-shirt, he seemed relaxed and friendly. The building on Francisco Street, which Mick's research on the Givenses had revealed he and Camilla owned, was a two-story stucco, flanked by much larger apartment houses. They lived on the top floor and rented out the lower unit.

Jay led me into a stark black-and-white room and offered me what he referred to as "the cow chair," a semi-recliner upholstered with black-and-white spotted cowhide and supported by a spindly faux-silver framework.

"It's the most comfortable chair in the place," he said.

I could believe that: the other furnishings looked as if they could be used as implements of torture. Apparently the Givenses had succumbed to every faddish object touted in popular publications' décor sections and the result was hideous. To make things worse, the windows that would have revealed a splendid view of the city lights were covered with draperies in a wild Hawaiian floral print.

Jay offered me coffee, and while he was in the kitchen, Camilla came out of a short hall that I assumed led to bedrooms. She wore a purple velveteen robe and had her hair wrapped in a towel.

"Sorry Jay's here. I knew you wanted our meeting to be private, but for once I couldn't get him to go about his nightly rounds — whatever they may be," she said, sitting down on a bright orange settee and thus creating another visual horror.

"I'm also sorry about being so casual," she went on. "I need to wash my hair early because it's so heavy and it takes so long to dry."

"I used to have long, heavy hair too."

She studied me. "Why'd you cut it?"

To disguise myself, I thought, remembering a particularly taxing case along the US-Mexican border. "It was more trouble than it was worth," I said.

"It suits you at shoulder length."

"Thanks."

Jay came in with two mugs of coffee and glanced questioningly at Camilla, who was lighting a cigarette.

"None for me," she said. "I won't sleep a wink."

I asked, "Is sleeplessness the reason for your late-night walks around the neighborhood?"

"Well . . . yes." She glanced quickly at her husband, then looked down at her hands. The fingers were twisted together, their knuckles white. She'd nearly crushed the freshly lit cigarette.

Jay didn't seem to notice his wife's unease, or if he did, his only reaction was to fiddle with an intricately woven silver bracelet on his right wrist. Vaguely I remembered he'd had on a different one the other day.

To keep things casual, I said, "Nice brace-let. I've been considering giving my husband one for his birthday, now that they've become fashionable for men."

"I hope he's more careful than Jay." Camilla cast him a dark look. "So far he's lost two — and they were expensive."

"And how many times have you lost expensive earrings or locked your keys in the car?" he shot back. "Repeated calls to Triple A cost too."

"They don't cost anything. Besides, every-body does that."

"I don't."

I put an end to the squabbling by saying, "I've drawn up an agency contract that you'll both need to read and sign."

I took two copies of the standard McCone Investigations agreement from my briefcase, handed one to each of them. Jay read slowly through his, but Camilla merely stared at the first page.

After a bit Jay said, "Looks okay to me." He scribbled a signature on it and offered it to Camilla, who signed too. "I'll get you a retainer check now," he added.

He hadn't bothered to ask his wife what she thought; Jay Givens clearly was the decision-maker in this twosome.

He went down the hall. When I was sure he was out of hearing range, I asked Camilla, "How are you holding up?"

"What does that mean?"

"Have you had any more bad experiences?"

"Bad experiences? That's a strange thing to call them. Of course *delusions, spells, nightmares, hallucinations* — they've all been applied to what's happened to me too." She paused, and in a plaintive voice asked, "Ms. McCone, do you believe I saw the things I say I did?"

"I wouldn't have taken the case if I didn't believe you saw *something.* Is there anything more you can tell me about them?"

"No." Quick glance at the hall down which her husband had disappeared.

"Any details you might have forgotten?"

"No, there's nothing." She paused. "Sometimes even I don't believe I saw what I did. Sometimes life . . . it's like a dream and I feel I can't get back to the place where I fell asleep so I can wake myself up."

"Have you talked with anybody about this? A therapist?"

"No. Jay doesn't . . . *we* don't believe in that kind of thing."

"What kind of thing, Cammie?" Jay had come down the hallway, check and contract in his hand.

"What?"

"You were telling Ms. McCone — Sharon — that we didn't believe in something."

"Oh, that." Briefly she closed her eyes. "Religion. We were talking about religion. Sharon's a Catholic, and I was going to tell her we were atheists." From under her half-lowered lids she flashed me a look of complicity.

Well, she was half right about my relationship with organized religion. I was raised Catholic, but lapsed somewhere along the way to adulthood. No rupture with the church, no big revelation about my faith — just a gradual process of attrition. To the grown-up me the world itself is too complex for its day-to-day issues to be understood; to contemplate a creator and his or her motivations for the full, and sometimes horrible, range of the human experience is impossible.

"What brought that subject up?" Jay asked.

"Just chatting." I put the contract and check in my briefcase. "Now that I'm officially representing you, I have a few questions to ask. Do either of you know the Kenyon brothers, Chad or Dick?"

They exchanged a glance, shook their heads.

"You must have heard of them. Your firm represents them, isn't that right, Jay?"

"Well, yes," he said, "but I've never met either one. It's a big firm, and there're many clients I never get to know. Besides, they're rich and powerful and surrounded by an army of gatekeepers."

"What about a man named Van Hoffman?"

"No," Camilla said. Jay hesitated before he echoed her.

I considered questioning them about the Night Searchers, but decided against it. Jay was inquisitive and would want to know why I'd asked and what the Searchers' connection to their case was. For all I knew there wasn't one. Maybe, if I got the opportunity, I'd ask Camilla, but right now she didn't seem particularly interested in anything outside her own little sphere.

"Well, I have what I need for now," I said, "so I'll leave you to the rest of your evening and report again tomorrow."

As I followed Jay to the door, I glanced back at Camilla: another emotion had crossed her face. It was fear. And I instinctively knew she was afraid of her husband.

10:02 p.m.

As I drove home, I thought about Camilla. She chattered a lot, and most people would have written her off as something of an airhead, but there were depths behind the ditzy façade. Also silences: it was what she *wasn't* saying that interested me, but hard as I tried, I couldn't get a handle on it. And that final fearful look: it was clear she didn't trust Jay, and I myself didn't like him very much, but he didn't seem to be a man who would do anyone serious harm. Then again, Camilla lived with him, and I didn't. To plumb the depths of those silences, I'd have to spend more time with her outside her husband's presence.

Hy still wasn't home when I got back to Avila Street, and there was no message on the foyer table where we usually left notes for each other. I ignored Alex and Jessie's pleadings for food while I checked my answering machine and flicked on the TV to see if any news of the Van Hoffman kidnapping had been leaked to the media. No, the lid was tightly on it — which meant less danger for all involved.

I hoped.

■ ■ ■ ■

THURSDAY,
MARCH 8

■ ■ ■ ■

6:10 a.m.

Hy called, as he often did, at an ungodly hour of the morning.

"Where the hell are you?" I snapped. And thought, *What a great start I've given to both our days.*

He laughed, however. "Des Moines. A —"

"— situation's come up," I finished for him. "What, your whereabouts aren't confidential any more?"

"I thought we'd settled that issue."

"It's just hard to get used to. Has anything happened with the Hoffman case?"

"Not a thing, dammit. No more communications, taunting or any other kind, from the kidnappers. McCone, can you spare some time to help me this morning? My people out there are tied up with other cases and —"

"Sure. What do you need?"

"For you to go down to Atherton and

73

interview Hoffman's wife and any family members you can locate. See if they can shed any light on the situation."

"Will do."

"E-mail me through RI if you find out anything useful."

11:33 a.m.

Atherton: an expensive, exclusive, leafy green community with a small downtown, nestled between the Bay and the Coastal Range on the Peninsula some thirty minutes south of the city. It was thickly wooded with pines and eucalyptus, and had large lots on winding lanes that discouraged high speeds. Nevertheless a group of helmeted, leather-clad motorcyclists on Harleys whipped around me as I was looking for the entrance to the Hoffman driveway on Isabella Avenue. I trailed my fingers in the air, and some of them waved back.

Mick has been riding Harleys for a number of years now. The machines have a bad reputation — Hell's Angels and too many movies like *Easy Rider* and *The Wild One* — and I admit I was leery at first when he bought his. But motorcyclists, like gun owners like me, are mostly conscientious, and Mick has been very careful. Except when he tried to fly off the Coast Highway after a

74

romantic disappointment — but that's a story better forgotten.

I drove past extensive properties, most of them walled and gated with only trees and roof peaks showing over their tops. Mick had found from his recent searches that the average home here sold for over four million dollars. The *average.* These properties in Atherton had probably been in families for generations — or in newly rich techies' hands for years or months — and they awed me.

When I reached the address for the Hoffmans' home and pulled into the driveway, I spotted an officer in an RI uniform sitting in a folding chair next to the wrought-iron gate. He was one of the men I knew, and he automatically waved me in.

The inner driveway, of red granite pebbles, skirted a lawn that was browned and weedy. At its top stood a French château–style house: smaller than its neighbors, with cream stucco walls fronted by mature yew trees. The walls needed repainting where the trees' branches had rubbed against them, one window to the right of the door was cracked, and there were shingles missing from the roof. Genteel neglect, because of financial problems?

I parked near the four-car garage and went

up the path to the front door. It opened before I could ring the bell, and a pair of faded green eyes, sunk deeply in their nests of wrinkles, peered out at me.

"Ms. McCone?"

"Yes." I offered my credentials, but the woman didn't glance at them. She must have had complete trust in the RI man on the gate.

"I'm Jane Hoffman," she said. "Come in, please."

She was very thin, with gray-blond hair cut in a page-boy that had gone out of style decades ago. Her skin had that leathery sheen of someone who has spent too much time worshiping the sun. Her hand, when she thrust it into mine, felt rough and dry.

"You must excuse me," she said, gesturing at her dark-blue sweat suit. "I've been too upset to dress —"

"I understand."

"We'll talk in the little room. I'll have Suzy bring us tea."

The "little room" was a den equipped with all the elements of leisurely living — wide-screen TV, pool table, brick fireplace, fifties-style jukebox — and overlooking an Olympic-sized swimming pool that was covered by a film of algae. Around the fireplace was a collection of furniture that conjured up an image of a rustic lake cottage. This, as indicated by a knitting bag, magazines, paperbacks, and sewing kit, was where Mrs. Hoffman spent her days.

"What a lovely room," I said, although it wasn't, particularly.

"Thank you. The children used to enjoy it, but of course they're grown now." She motioned me to one of the armchairs and bellowed in an unexpectedly loud voice, "Suzy! Tea!"

"I have to yell at her," Mrs. Hoffman told me with a confiding look. "She's my great-niece, Suzy Cushing, a college girl. All that music through the headphones — it makes them deaf."

More likely that *she* would make Suzy deaf.

Suzy was cute — Texas cute, as Mick would say. Blond and curvy and perky, like a cheerleader. When she set the tray down she spoke in a foreign language I couldn't quite place.

"Show-off," Mrs. Hoffman grumbled.

Suzy smiled. "I'm a linguistics minor at Stanford, with a major in geopolitical physics. What I just said was Nepali for 'I hope you enjoy your repast.'"

"And this degree will allow you to . . . ?"

"Delve into the way we humans — in

many nations and languages — have contrived to fuck this planet."

"Suzy! No F words!"

The young woman left the room, laughing.

Mrs. Hoffman was laughing too. "That one," she said, "can put a smile on my face no matter how bad I feel."

"I've got a couple of those in my family," I told her, thinking of Mick and his younger sister Jamie. "But as to the current circumstances . . ."

"Yes." The smile disappeared and she spooned some sugar into her tea. "Mr. Ripinsky recommends you highly."

"I have to qualify his praise: I'm also his wife."

"He explained that to me, and I'm happy to see an example of how times have changed. In my day — and I suppose to this day in my generation — a husband would never praise his wife for her professional abilities, much less work together with her. He'd be proud of her volunteer work or her cake baking or her fine sewing, perhaps, but nothing more serious. Like Van used to be proud of me."

I caught a bitter twist to her words. Well, I couldn't blame her. She struck me as intelligent and capable — someone who might

78

have done well in many fields of endeavor.

I took out my tape recorder. "Do you mind? I'm a bad notetaker."

"Please, go ahead."

I switched it on, and gave the date and time and nature of the interview.

"First of all," I said, "has there been any ransom demand?"

"There has, by phone at eight thirty this morning."

"Did you take the call?"

"Yes."

"Was the caller's voice familiar?"

"I can't say. It was distorted."

"Male? Female?"

"It was impossible to tell."

"How much did the caller demand?"

"Forty-five thousand dollars."

"Did you — or are you going to — pay it?"

"Certainly not! That amount is almost exactly what we have in savings. If my husband doesn't return, it's all I'll have to live on for the rest of my life."

"But this house —"

"It's mortgaged for more than I could sell it for. And my husband's position is about to be abolished. At best, what the two of us can hope for is spending the rest of our days in some tiny, wretched apartment."

79

"Does Mr. Hoffman have life insurance?"

"Not any more. He let it lapse."

A grim picture for her, from any angle.

"Let's talk about your husband. Would you say his work can be dangerous?"

"Van is a philosopher. He advises governments and private individuals on how to deal with global conflicts. Dangerous? I suppose it might be."

"He's in a position that would allow him access to information of national security?"

". . . I really don't know. He never talks about his work."

"You called RI when he didn't come home at the expected time. You must have thought something was wrong."

"Not really. I called them because that was what Van has always told me to do in what might be a crisis situation."

"But you weren't seriously concerned for his safety?"

"Well, no. In the thirty-six years we've been married, he's never before given me cause to worry."

"This is an awkward question, but I have to ask it: is there any possibility that he may be seeing another woman?"

"Of course not! My husband has always been completely faithful. He's away from home a lot, but he leaves contact numbers in case I need him."

"Only not this time."

"No, not this time."

"To your knowledge, does he have any personal enemies?"

She paused, but her eyes never left mine. I'd seen that kind of hesitation before: coolly calculating, judging how far a lie can go.

"None that I can think of, no."

I shifted the focus slightly. "From my research, I see that your husband used to maintain a public presence, and was very outspoken about his policy recommendations. Then, about a year ago, all that changed. Now he rarely gives interviews, avoids the press. Why?"

"I . . . don't know. Are you sure that he's changed?"

"You haven't noticed it?"

". . . As I said before, he doesn't talk to me about his work. We have separate lives. I have my own activities — charities, you know — and, well, they take up a great deal of my time."

"You mentioned that your children are grown?"

"Yes, we have two: Melinda and Catharine. Melinda is a stay-at-home mom. Catharine is a . . . career woman." Faint disapproval in the last statement.

"What does Catharine do?"

"She and a friend own the BodyWorks, that exclusive spa in Palo Alto."

"Is she married?"

"No. Ms. McCone, exactly where is all this going?"

"I'm trying to get a sense of what your family is like."

"It's my husband who's gone missing, not the rest of my family!"

The phone shrilled. Mrs. Hoffman looked at it apprehensively, as if afraid it might be bad news.

Someone, probably Suzy, answered it on an extension. After a moment the red message light stopped blinking.

"A wrong number," Mrs. Hoffman said in relieved tones. "We've had a lot of those lately. Is there anything else?"

"Do you know the Givenses of San Francisco, Camilla and Jay?"

". . . The names are not familiar."

"What about the Kenyon brothers, Dick and Chad?"

Her nose wrinkled. "I've heard of them. I guess most people have. What do they have to do with my husband's disappearance?"

"Perhaps nothing. Are you sure your husband has never had dealings with them?"

"How would I know?" She put her hands over her eyes. "Ms. McCone, I'm so tired. If you'll leave a contract for your services, I'll return it with a retainer check tomorrow morning."

"There's no need for that: I'm working for RI. The Global Policy Forum pays their bill."

"Oh, yes, of course. For now, would you please excuse me?"

Without waiting for a reply, she stood with difficulty and left the room. I waited a moment and then went looking for Suzy.

12:15 p.m.

A thin, nervous-looking woman who was chopping vegetables in the kitchen informed me that Suzy was in the potting shed. She directed me through a door to a small, shingled structure nestled under the boughs of a pine tree.

"I thought you'd want to talk with me," Suzy said, dusting soil from her fingers. "Tomatoes," she added. "I'm a little slow getting them started, but they fruit in late August."

"So in addition to being a geophysicist and a linguist, you're also a gardener."

She drew up a stool, motioned me to a second one. "Dealing with plants relaxes

83

me. That's a definite plus in this household."

"Mind if I ask how come you're living here?"

"I promised my mom I'd look after Aunt Jane. It was part of the deal for Mom and Dad footing my tuition at Stanford."

"Your aunt Jane has a husband. Can't he be depended on to look after her?"

"Well, hardly. He's never here even when he is, if you know what I mean. And Aunt Jane's pretty fragile. A stroke, three years ago. She's all right now, but she needs somebody."

"I see."

"I don't think you do. The stroke affected her emotionally. She cries frequently and at length for no good reason. She blanks out, stares at nothing for hours. She's afraid to drive. It's difficult to even get her to go out of the house. Personally, I think Uncle Van's neglect is slowly driving her crazy."

"What do you think has happened to him?"

"I don't have any idea. Nothing terrible, I hope — in spite of him being a bastard."

"What about his work? Would you say there's any danger in it?"

"I certainly wouldn't. He sits in his office and ponders issues that have no clear connection to reality. He writes reports that are probably ignored. Frankly, I think he might welcome some kind of danger; at least he'd feel alive. He walks around here like a character out of *Night of the Living Dead*."

"And he's not often home?"

"No, he stays away long hours — often up to twenty a day. Personally, I think he spends most of those hours playing solitaire on his computer and devising other ways to keep from having to come home. After all, he's got a do-nothing job with a do-nothing foundation that Washington is about to ax. When he gets back from the office, he collapses on the couch in his study." Suzy frowned. "But, you know, after some of those late nights, he gets up acting jazzed as hell and cooks himself up a huge breakfast."

"Jazzed — how?"

"Chipper — as chipper as a man of his temperament can be. Self-satisfied, as if he'd scored big-time. Maybe he *does* have another woman."

"I see. About this forty-five-thousand-dollar ransom — is it really true that she can't pay it?"

"Oh, she could pay it if she wanted to."

"She claims it's nearly all they have in their savings account."

"So? There're stocks, bonds, retirement accounts. She just doesn't want to pay it, is

85

all. You might not believe it to look at her, but Aunt Jane is keeper of the financial keys in this household. And rightly so — most of the money was hers to begin with."

"So your uncle might not know how much they're worth?"

Suzy smiled wickedly. "He only knows what Aunt Jane wants him to. And that's not much."

"You seem to have a very firm grasp on what goes on in this family."

"What can I say? I've got excellent hearing and an acute case of nosiness. I'll tell you this: they're dysfunctional as hell. Make my family look like Beaver Cleaver's."

I grinned at that. "Well, keep your ears fine-tuned. Will you give me contact information for Melinda and Catharine?"

She rattled off addresses and phone numbers from memory, and I scribbled them down.

I asked, "You'll keep me informed if you hear anything?"

"I will." She reached for the paper on which I'd written the two numbers. "That's for my cell, if you need to talk with me again."

"Thanks. Let me know if there're any phone calls from your uncle. And if anything else isn't right here, anything at all, please tell the guard."

"Of course."

When I left the potting shed, Suzy was wiping dirt off her hands onto her grubby jeans.

1:11 p.m.

Palo Alto has always held a strong attraction for me. Although it is the home of Stanford University and currently the center of the now-reviving tech and venture capital markets, it still seems, with its quiet treelined streets and friendly people, to offer a pleasant contrast with the hustle and aggressiveness of Silicon Valley.

I found BodyWorks, co-owned by Catharine Hoffman, down an alley off University Avenue, where ivy and other vines twined over aged bricks. It was a stately building dating from California's golden era — possibly the 1880s — but its Revival period façade had been spoiled by the addition of large windows behind which men and women of various sizes and shapes climbed StairMasters, strode along treadmills, and pumped stationary bikes.

As I opened the door, the clump of feet and grunts and groans came to my ears. I stopped in the middle of the entry and looked to my right, where a dance class was in session. To my left, a dozen or more people were performing tai chi. A honey-blond woman with a cordial smile greeted me from behind a lectern-style desk.

"You are here for . . . ?" she asked.

"Catharine Hoffman."

"And you are . . . ?"

I handed her one of my cards. "Please take it to her. I called a while ago, and she's expecting me."

I waited, wondering if the lack of anything resembling a chair in the lobby was intended to keep the clients on their feet and moving even before their classes began. This spa, with its soft recessed lighting, pastel walls, and — I saw from discreet signs posted at the hallways that branched off toward the rear — a juice bar and swimming pool, was a far cry from the rehab center where I'd gone after my bout with locked-in syndrome. A far cry from the private gym where I now worked out two or three times a week with my friend Piper, whom I'd met in rehab.

Not that my gym was such a bad thing. In these surroundings I would have lolled in the pool or idled at the juice bar. I still needed a considerable boot in the butt to get myself going, and the attendants there were only too glad to provide it.

After a few minutes the woman returned and said, "Ms. Hoffman will see you in her office. Go down the first hallway to the left, turn to the right. Last door on the left."

I followed her directions, over deep carpet and past walls hung with innocuous pastels of wild flowers, and knocked on the door. A husky voice told me to come in.

The light in the office was pale lavender. The scent that tickled my nostrils was also lavender. A tall woman in violet sweats and a baseball cap was standing behind a maple desk, my card in her hand. As I got closer, I saw her features were very like her mother's.

"Ms. McCone," she said. "You said on the phone that you're working on my father's disappearance."

"Yes."

"Sit down, please."

I did, and she sat at the desk.

"I assume that if you'd found out anything you'd have said so."

"I've found very little so far. There have been various e-mails, none of them amounting to much, and piggybacked off different accounts. Do you know of anybody who would want to harm your father?"

She hesitated, choosing her words carefully. "Any number of people. He isn't a particularly likable man."

"Why is that?"

Shrug. "For one thing, he's into power. Likes to dominate anyone he perceives as weaker than himself. For another, he's a womanizer. And for a third, he's a lousy father."

"What about people who are stronger and more powerful than him? How does he treat them?"

"He either acts indifferent or kisses ass."

"Who would those individuals be?"

"Politicians — local, state, and national. The board members of the Forum. Wealthy businessmen who make contributions or give him stock tips."

"Insiders' tips?"

"I suppose so. He hasn't done very well, though. His sense of timing is off."

"Any women among them?"

"No, my father dislikes and distrusts women. As far as he's concerned, we're all here to be used in one way or another."

"So, in short, there're a lot of people who might want to harm him?"

"A lot. Including me." She held up her hand like a crossing guard. "But no, I didn't. I've severed my life from his, gotten on with things."

"What about your mother? She seemed omewhat protective of him."

"It's an act. She's the one who holds financial power. For a long time he hadn't figured that out, but I guess he finally did. At least he started staying out late at night a year or so ago, against her wishes. She claims he's involved in 'spy activities.' So far, no one's been able to dislodge the idea and get her to face up to the obvious."

"Which is?"

"What does any insecure middle-aged man who feels whatever power he once had is slipping away do?"

"Has an affair. You have any proof of it?"

Catharine shook her head. "Just a suspicion, is all."

"Why does your father feel he's losing his grip on power?"

"I only know what I read in the papers and on the Net. Public contributions to the Forum are down, so is governmental support. Not a single relevant idea on public policy has come out of there in years. The current administration in D.C. is considering setting up its own advisory boards in various regions of the country. Then, I'm afraid, my father and his cohorts will be forcibly retired."

I made a note to learn more about the situation. I was getting conflicting stories, about both Hoffman and the Forum.

"Would you say he's in financial difficulty?"

"That I wouldn't know. He may be; Mom isn't."

"The house in Atherton seems run-down."

"Does it? I haven't been there in a long time."

"Not even to see your mother?"

"No. She has Suzy; she doesn't need me."

"You don't like Suzy."

"Actually I do. She's funny and bright, and she takes good care of Mom. Keeps her off my back, you might say."

"So it's your mother you don't like."

"No law says you have to like your mother."

I stood, thinking how good it was to like both my mothers. "You've been very kind to give me so much of your time, Ms. Hoffman. I'll be speaking to your sister next."

"Melinda?" She looked startled.

"Yes. Is there something wrong — ?"

"I'd prefer to let you form your own conclusions about my sister."

2:25 p.m.
Melinda Campton's house was in a crumbling old subdivision on the outskirts of Millbrae, about three-quarters of the way between Palo Alto and the city. Most of the

sixties ranch-style homes needed paint; their yards were weedy and largely unbarbered. Discarded toys skulked in the weeds, cars stood helplessly on blocks, and a couple of garbage cans were overturned, spilling refuse into the street.

The woman who answered my ring had blank gray eyes and a slack jaw. There were bruises on her cheeks and forearms. I could see some faint resemblance to her sister and mother, but not much.

"Unnnh?" she grunted, tucking a strand of dirty, blond hair behind her ear.

"You're Melinda Campton?"

"Yes. Who're you?"

"Sharon McCone. I called earlier."

"You're the one who's looking for *him*. Van. The asshole."

"May I come in so we can talk?"

". . . I guess."

I stepped into a living room that was cluttered beyond belief: newspapers and junk mail strewn everywhere; dirty glasses and dishes and ashtrays balanced on tables and chair arms. The air reeked of stale cigarette smoke. Melinda went straight to an old recliner chair, flipped its leg rest up, and lit a cigarette. For a moment, inhaling deeply, she seemed to have forgotten I was there.

Deeply disturbed. Abused, definitely.

Mentally challenged? Emotionally, anyway.

I said, "Do you have any idea what might've happened to your father?"

"No."

"You know it's possible he was abducted."

"Who'd want him?"

"You tell me."

"Well, it can't be for money. He doesn't have any. He gambles everything away on the stock market. I asked him to pay for this life skills class at the community college — so I could be a better mother to my kids, you know? You want to see pictures of them?"

Before I could reply, she got up and fetched a couple of framed photos from the mantel over the fake fireplace.

"That's Janey, she's named after my mother." A towhead of about six with an incipient frown and thin, stern lips.

"And this is Roseanne, after the TV actress, you know?" Another towhead, this one around eight, jaw thrust out aggressively, fierce little eyes.

"Lovely children," I lied.

"Yeah, they are." Melinda thumped the photos back onto the mantel and herself into the recliner. "They're the best, but I haven't been dealing too well with them since their asshole dad left. Emptied our bank account and took off in the car. Mom and Cat — that's my sister — have helped with the rent, and I'm hoping to get a job real soon, but in the meantime I've kind of been taking things out on my kids, and I thought this life skills class . . . well, it's only fifty dollars for the quarter, so I asked my father if he'd pay for it, and he said he was broke."

I thought of the shabby condition of the house in Atherton, the run-down grounds. And Van Hoffman's playing unsuccessfully in the stock market, the public policy institute that was about to go under. Still, Jane Hoffman had money.

"Did you ask your mother for the fifty dollars?"

"My mother? Are you kidding? She *hates* me."

"Why?"

"Because I'm not the perfect person she wants me to be. And she hates Cat — my sister — because she's successful."

What kind of woman, I wondered, hates her children for both their flaws and their assets?

"What about asking Cat?"

"I can't. Cat would want payback."

"Of what sort?"

"She'd tell me to get my act together, take

95

care of my kids, get some education, a job . . . all that shit."

"That doesn't sound so bad to me."

"To you, maybe. You look like somebody who's had a pretty good life. But when you're like me, beaten up by my own husband, then it's a whole different story."

Melinda was watching me, assessing my reaction. I kept my voice neutral as I said, "Okay, I understand. But maybe somebody wanted information from your father? Classified information?"

"Nah. That forum doesn't keep secrets; they publish their reports. My dad isn't important to anybody."

"I've heard he's not home a lot, sometimes stays out all night."

"He's got a woman. I've met her. Who cares? At least he's not around to give Mom and Suzy grief."

"What kind of grief?"

"Threats, tantrums. Once he broke Mom's wrist, and another time he slammed Suzy against a wall."

Yet another conflicting report. How much credence should I give it — or any of the others? If it was true Suzy was there to protect her aunt Jane from her uncle Van, why hadn't she confided that to me?

"Did either of them report the incidents

to the police?"

Melinda turned her head to one side, but I could see the flush rising across her neck and cheek. "That doesn't help. The cops come out, they're nice, sometimes they throw the guy — like my Tony — in jail and you can take out a restraining order. But a piece of paper isn't gonna keep somebody who wants to hurt you away for long. Tony was back, and back, and back. Especially on my paydays."

"Where's Tony now?"

"I don't know. After a while he probably found somebody else who had a bigger paycheck than me."

"And this woman your dad has — who is she?"

"Her name's Pamela. I met her once. They were sitting at an outdoor café in Palo Alto, and I saw them and went over to say hello. Dad was embarrassed — no, horrified. I guess I'm not fit to be his daughter. But he introduced us, although he didn't ask me to sit down. She was nice. He doesn't deserve her."

"Did you catch her last name?"

She scrunched her eyes closed, then shook her head.

"What did she look like?"

"Long black hair, pretty."

"Do you remember anything else about her?"

". . . She looked expensive. Nice clothes, nice fingernails. She looked like I could never look." Her face crumpled and tears began to flow. "He doesn't deserve her, but he thinks I don't deserve him."

There was nothing I could say to comfort her.

Melinda said, "I think I'd like to be alone now."

I put my card on the table beside her and left.

4:38 p.m.

When I arrived at the RI building, I first e-mailed the report on the Hoffman situation that I'd promised Hy, emphasizing the conflicting stories on the man's life and character that I'd received from his family members. Then I went to speak with Mick. He was on the phone, scribbling notes in the self-developed shorthand only he could read. He held up a hand, pointed to a chair.

"Uh-huh," he said. "Duck confit. Isn't that a little passé? I mean, they're eating it in the burbs now."

On my time, on a company phone line, the food snob was talking to a restaurant! I stepped forward, pressed the disconnect button.

Mick turned wounded eyes to me. "Shar, do you *know* how long it takes to get through to Clos Bob, much less to make a reservation?"

"It's a stupid name for a restaurant. Besides, I read a review of it; they'll probably close within the year." I flopped into the chair, added, "I can remember when McDonald's suited you just fine."

He hesitated, then grinned. "Still does."

"You have anything to tell me besides that duck confit is passé?"

"This Treasure Hunting game — it's getting interesting."

"Tell me more about them," I said.

Mick settled back into his conversational posture — leaning back in his chair, feet propped on an open desk drawer. "They're a loosely knit national organization, brought together on the Internet. Each 'chapter,' as they call them, has a different name; in this city it's the Night Searchers. In New York it's the Canyon Creepers. In L.A. it's the Smog Skimmers. You get the drift."

"Right," I said, ignoring the unintentional pun.

"All the information," Mick went on, "except for real names, addresses, and so forth, is right out there. You tap into their website, where times and starting places for the hunts are posted."

"Do you have to sign up with them, or what?"

"No. You just show up. It's all anonymous."

"And what is the purpose of these hunts?"

"Well, there's a prize, usually something of considerable value, donated by the 'hider' for that particular game. But I think the real motivation is the creeping around, the danger of getting caught where you're not supposed to be. That's the real deal."

"You ever been on one of these hunts?"

"No, but I've met people who have."

"You want to go on one?"

"I've got the feeling I will, whether I want to or not."

"Look up when the next one is."

He swiveled to his keyboard. "Tomorrow night at seven thirty, starting in the Panhandle. A map is included."

I hesitated. There was a possibility I'd run into Jay Givens if I went along, but the possibility of his finding my presence suspicious was greatly outweighed by the possibility of learning something. I said, "Print out two, in case we get separated."

"D'you suppose," Mick said, "that these

Night Searchers have something to do with that vacant lot on Saturn Street?"

"Possibly. Were you able to line up appointments with the owners for me?" Earlier I'd texted him and asked him to do so.

"The Kenyon brothers, Chad and Dick, have more gatekeepers than President Obama. Their people say they'll check with the Kenyons and call back, but they don't call back — you know the routine. But there's a weak spot in the gate — Chad. He's a creature of habit, seldom varies his personal routines, dismisses his 'keepers,' as he calls them, when his private time begins."

"So it wouldn't be too difficult for someone to locate and approach him."

"Right."

"He married?"

"Nope, but he likes the ladies. In particular, beautiful Latinas."

"Perfect."

"Shar, what're you up to?"

"I'm not 'up to' anything at all. If Julia's still in the office, would you ask her to come in here?"

5:15 p.m.
Julia Rafael, a tall, strong-featured Hispanic woman whose shining black hair was today swept up on top of her head and secured

101

with abalone-shell combs, swept into my office and flopped into one of the visitors' chairs.

"*Dios mio,* what a day!" she exclaimed. "And now I suppose you're going to heap more *cagada* on me."

When she'd first come to the agency, she'd never have talked to me in such a manner. A former teenage prostitute who had done time in the California Youth Authority, she had been turned around by the birth of her son, Tonio, and she'd been determined to make a good, if stilted, impression on a prospective employer. After months of working at the agency — months of hearing and seeing how the rest of us spoke and interacted — she'd finally let her real persona shine through. It was a persona we were all happy with.

"Yes, but this is the kind of shit you might not be too unhappy with."

"Oh? What now?"

"A surveillance. Chad Kenyon. The details are in this folder." I pushed it toward her.

She scanned it. "You sure I'm the right person for this? High roller, pricey haunts?"

"And a weakness for beautiful Hispanic women — or so Mick says. Grab something glitzy from the property room" — what we called the closet where we kept an assort-

102

ment of clothing to suit anyone from a beggar to a socialite — "and keep track of him."

"Contact? No contact?"

"Either. The closer you can get to him, the better. If you make actual contact, try to find out the points I've outlined in the file."

"Will do."

"I forgot to ask: is Tonio covered tonight?" Even though Julia lived with her sister, who cared for her son in her absence, I was concerned about him.

Julia smiled archly. "Tonio is going to the movies with my friend Joseph tonight, and then staying over at his apartment."

"Who's Joseph?"

"Boss, you haven't been listening to the office gossip these days."

She winked at me as she left my office.

6:01 p.m.
I poured myself a glass of wine and sat in my armchair, contemplating strategy, then went back to my desk and began listening to messages and making calls.

Hy: "Nothing yet on the VH matter. I'm still working the situation in Des Moines, but we're close to a resolution. Love you."

Julia's cell was turned off. She was already on the trail of Chad Kenyon.

103

None of Mick's numbers answered.

Duck confit, I thought. *Uh-huh.*

Derek Ford, my other techie, was at home — surprisingly. Of course, it was too early for him to hit the restaurants and clubs he enjoyed.

"Sure," he said, "I can run those checks in no time. Let me see if I've got them straight: Chad Kenyon, Dick Kenyon. The Global Policy Forum. Anything else?"

"Not for now."

"Call if you think of anything."

"What, you're not going out?"

"I am" — he made a mock sobbing noise — "disappointed in love."

"What happened? And with whom?"

"Can't remember. Now that I've got work to do, I'm over it."

I clicked the phone off, smiling.

My other operatives were working cases I'd assigned to them: Patrick Neilan, a single father with sole custody of his boys, was after a deadbeat dad — his favorite kind of hunt. Craig Morland and Adah Joslyn — he a former FBI agent, she a former SFPD homicide investigator, and recently married to each other — had taken on an overnight surveillance of a woman suspected of insurance fraud.

I might as well go down the Embarcadero

to Carmen's, one of the last few waterfront diners, for a bite to eat.

8:03 p.m.
The diner had seen better days. Its original owner, a former longshoreman, had been a good cook and a genial host, plying his customers with tales of the old waterfront when San Francisco had been a true seafaring port, before the shipping business decamped to more modernized facilities across the Bay in Oakland. When he retired, the diner passed through the hands of various owners, and with each one the food and service grew worse. Now the leatherette booths were cracked and bleeding stuffing, the Formica tables were gouged with drawings and initials, and one of the windows overlooking the water was badly cracked. Sometimes I wondered why I even bothered to go there.

Well, I supposed because the waterfront diners were a dying breed: only a handful of them still existed. As with the piers, many had been torn down or replaced by boutique shops and expensive restaurants. But even with today's public art, new sports stadium, and upscale businesses, part of the waterfront was dying. The hundreds of palm trees that had been planted on the median strip after the 1989 Loma Prieta earthquake were succumbing to a contagious fungal disease called Fusarium wilt, which is almost always fatal. Many would live on for years, and the city planned to replace those that didn't survive with a hardier species, but it would never be the same. Just as the rough-and-tumble Barbary Coast had vanished. And the steamship age. And a lot of other things that had made this city unique.

Enough, McCone!

At Carmen's I took the least disreputable of the booths and ordered a cheeseburger — rare, since it would come out overcooked anyway, but maybe that way the cook wouldn't incinerate it quite as much. It arrived well done, with a slab of American cheese oozing over the sides. I ate it anyway. No sending food back at Carmen's.

I was the sole patron except for a very old man — known only as Micah — whom I'd occasionally used as an informant. He ignored me. No skulduggery on the waterfront, nothing to sell, therefore I didn't exist. Fine with me. He was unpleasant and demanding, and his information was often inaccurate. I paid the check and started for the door, but then he hissed at me.

For a moment I almost didn't turn around. When I did, he beckoned for me to come closer.

"Was a guy askin' around about you to-day."

"A guy."

"Big, ugly guy. Smelled funny — like lime juice. Seemed to me that he thought you was still at the pier."

"He tell you his name?"

"Hell no."

"Say why he wanted to see me?"

"Nope. Wasn't up to no good, I bet."

"Why do you say that?"

"Somethin' about the way he asked. I dunno. What do I look like — a shrink?"

"You tell him where I'd gone?"

"How could I? How would I know?"

"Thanks for telling me." I dug in my bag, handed him a five.

"Twenty'd be better."

"Five's what it's worth. You see him again, you find out more, then we'll talk money."

"Stingy bitch," he muttered.

I walked away.

Big, ugly guy who smelled like lime juice.
Well, that could fit any number of men in this city. I thought about the Givens case and the Hoffman inquiry I'd taken on for Hy. No big ugly guys associated with either.

Wasn't up to no good.

A disgruntled former client, like the man

who had hired the arsonist who torched my home on Church Street? Somebody whom I'd caused to be arrested and testified against? You made enemies in this business, and even if they were incarcerated there was no guarantee that they wouldn't be out on the streets again seeking vengeance. Nothing to do but stay alert.

Might as well head home. The cats would be hungry, and maybe there was something watchable on TV.

9:13 p.m.

On the way to the garage I changed my mind, and against my better judgment decided to go by the lot on Saturn Street again. I paused to admire my new car before I got in. When my BMW Z4 — sold to me by Rae, since Ricky insisted on buying her a new car every year on her birthday — was destroyed in the house fire, I'd been devastated. For years I'd driven and loved an old MG I'd owned since college, but I'd loved the Z4 even more. For a while I drove rentals, and then Hy surprised me with a Mercedes SLK 350 roadster. Red, with a removable hardtop and a black ragtop.

At first I'd thought the car was too showy for someone in my position, but Hy explained it was the opposite: nobody would believe that an investigator would drive such a sporty machine. Besides, the car was powerful enough that I could easily lose the most determined of pursuers. All my life I've had love affairs with cars, but this was the biggie.

I took what I thought of as my "skulking clothes" from the trunk, and went back to the office to put them on. Then I drove to Russian Hill, parking even farther away than I had before. Darted for the shadows of the overhang where I'd waited on my previous visit, and checked out the area for pedestrians or people at windows. There were none, but from the pit I heard low voices, their words indistinct.

An icy wind whistled above the excavation and was sucked down in a vortex. Not a good place for anyone to take shelter tonight. As I stood in the shadows, I heard a moan, and then a gruff voice said, "We better get outta here. A doorway's better than this."

"But the baby . . ."

In a moment two figures appeared from the darkness through the hole in the fence and emerged onto the sidewalk. They didn't see me as they huddled together. The woman was obviously pregnant and close to term.

"Where're we goin' to go, honey?" Her voice was tremulous; she was trying not to cry.

"Wherever. At least we're still together."

I thought quickly, then turned on my flashlight and approached them. They froze like a pair of frightened deer caught in the glare of headlights.

"What were you two doing down there?" I asked in a brusque, official voice.

"Nothing, ma'am. Just lookin' for shelter till this wind stops." He raised his hand at the sky.

"Have you sheltered there before?"

"Twice, maybe three times. But that was in the fall when it was warmer."

"Did you see anybody else tonight?"

They both shook their heads.

"Only fools like us would try it in this weather," the man said. "Like I was tellin' her when we climbed out, even a doorway's better than down there."

"Okay. You know we usually arrest people for trespassing on this lot, but in weather like this . . . well. I'm not going to hassle you. In fact, I'll help you people out."

"Why would you do that?"

I thought of Joey McCone, dead of a drug overdose in a rain-soaked shack near Eureka.

110

"Let's just say I once had a brother who was in a fix like yours."

"What happened to him?" the woman asked softly.

"He died. I don't want that to happen to either of you — or your baby."

The woman closed her eyes; the man cleared his throat gruffly.

I dug in my pocket, pulled out what cash I had there. Didn't count it — it wasn't much, but enough to help people with none at all. Added my business card to it.

"Take this. If you need any more help, get hold of me."

After a hesitation, the man took it. "Thank you."

"Better get going; there's a rainstorm supposed to blow in soon."

When they were gone, I slipped through the fence and descended carefully by the light of my flash. The pit was the same desolate, post-apocalyptic scene as before: slabs of broken concrete, discarded household items, rags and cans and other trash. But this time I noticed something new: the top to a refrigerator's vegetable crisper, snapped in half. I had one like it, and I'd long yearned to exert the same violence upon it.

Slowly I prowled the bottom of the pit,

looking for . . . what? I wasn't sure. In a cleared area near the center were the remains of a fire, not the same remains I'd seen on my previous visit. I shone the flashlight on charred wood stained with drippings. There was no evidence of a pot of any sort, much less an iron one suitable for boiling an infant. I squatted down, leaned closer, sniffing. Bacon. Other meat odors. Something sweet. What . . . ? Marshmallows. Even the homeless were entitled to a treat once in a while —

I picked up a stick and stirred through the charred wood pieces. Something glinted among them. I poked at it. A piece of metal with a small bit of leather attached to one end. I placed it in one of the plastic bags I keep in my "skulking clothes" for collecting evidence, then stirred the wood and ashes some more. Next, a cigarette lighter — gold, expensive-looking, probably a Dunhill. What the hell was that doing here?

Well, one of the homeless people might have found or stolen it, then dropped it while lighting a fire. I flipped the lid and flicked the control on its side: it didn't work; the wick and elements looked burned out. Maybe tossed away by someone who didn't know they could be replaced? Or couldn't afford to replace them? It went into another bag.

There were remnants of long matches such as you use to start fireplaces or barbecues; a ballpoint pen with the name of its supplier obliterated; a segment of a thick ornamental gold cord; a paper clip chain, the clips in the shape of dog bones; a buckle that looked as if it might have come from a watchband. You never know, so all of that went into baggies too.

Clang!

Something struck a sheet of metal close to my head. Instinctively I turned the flash off and dropped to the ground, covering my head. The object thrown from above hadn't sounded large. A beer can, maybe?

Another clang. Definitely a can of some sort.

Silence. Probably whoever had done the throwing wasn't aiming at me. Just another refuse dumper.

We're becoming a nation of slobs.

No sooner had I gotten to my feet than my cell vibrated. I pulled it from my pocket, checked the number. Ma.

For God's sake, not again! Not now!

I switched the phone off, knowing there would be hell to pay when I returned the call.

I'd been there in the pit long enough. Carefully I made my way to street level, clutching the top edge and peering up and down the street before I pulled myself up and headed for my car.

11:20 p.m.
The landline was ringing when I stepped into our new house.

Not Ma again!

The machine clicked on and announced that the parties it served were not available.

The caller was my sister Charlene Christiansen, in Bel Air, outside of L.A. Mick's mother, Ricky's former wife. The smart one, with a PhD in international finance and a thriving career. But first and foremost a mother — she was devoted to her six kids.

"What's the matter with Ma?" she asked when I picked up. "She's driving me crazy!"

"I got the message about the show with her paintings in it, but that can't be the trouble. What's she upset about now?"

"That Patsy has, quote, gone and done it again, unquote."

Patsy is the family's youngest, a chef and restaurant owner currently living in the Napa Valley. She also has three kids by three different fathers, and it wouldn't have surprised me if earth mother Patsy wanted

114

a fourth.

"So what's Ma's problem? Pats can support any number of kids."

"Ma finds it 'unseemly.' "

"What's unseemly is Ma objecting. She loves her grandkids. She's always after Hy and me to give her another one."

"That's because you don't have any. Have too many and — pow! — you're in trouble."

She ought to know. I said, "I suppose you want me to talk to Ma."

"Would you? Please? Pretty please?"

"Maybe. What'll you give me?"

"What's that supposed to mean?"

"I don't do family stuff for nothing, you know."

"Bitch. What do you want?"

"Free tickets to a Cheryl Wheeler concert."

"I'm sure Ricky can score some. Just ask him."

"No, *you* ask him."

"If this is about my reluctance to ask favors from my ex-husband —"

"There's a concert coming up in Boulder this June. I haven't seen the Rockies in ages."

"You want plane fare."

"For two. And when I'm in Denver, I love to stay at the Brown Palace."

"Mercenary!"

"Oh, and there's this great little restaurant that serves the most amazing duck —"

"Bitch!"

"Beloved sister, whom I'm saving from a very uneasy conversation —"

"Okay, you talk with Ma. I'll foot the bill for your vacation." Charlene's voice softened. "Besides," she added, "this mess of a family owes you more than you can imagine."

Before I called Ma, I decided to call Patsy. She was a hands-on restaurateur who would be there until the last dish was washed and the last dime counted.

"Villa Napoli," a chipper female voice said.

"Patsy McCone, please."

"Ms. Patsy is busy right now."

I knew very well what Ms. Patsy was doing at this hour: relaxing with a glass — or three — of wine after the evening rush. "Tell her to get off her butt and talk with her sister."

"Yes, ma'am."

In a minute Patsy came on the line. "Which sister?" she asked.

"The oldest one."

"Shar! How are you?"

"Fine. How're you?"

"Couldn't be better."

I cut to the chase. "Ma says you've 'gone and done it again.' Are you pregnant?"

"God, is that all the family can give me credit for? I happen to have bought a new restaurant. In Sonoma."

"That's great! What about Villa Napoli?"

"It'll go on. I've hired an excellent manager."

"So you're moving to Sonoma?"

"I am. Watch out, Shar, I'm getting closer and closer to you every year."

Sonoma wasn't all that much closer to the city than Napa. "I'll worry about that when you buy down here."

"Actually, I've got my sights set on a pretty good location there too."

We chatted for a while about her kids, her current boyfriends — always plural these days — and Hy and me. Then I explained about Ma's complaints to Charlene, which she promised to straighten out — leaving me free of further late-night conversation.

I regarded the ziplocks I'd offloaded onto the kitchen table when I'd come in. Then I got a section of newspaper from the recycle bin and emptied the bags onto it. Pretty slim pickings.

The gold cigarette lighter was the only valuable item. I checked it over, found it wouldn't light — although it did give off an unpleasant butane stink — but I couldn't imagine anybody throwing out such an expensive lighter as if it were a disposable Bic. I'd have it checked by Richman Labs for residual contents and prints tomorrow and then have them messenger it to the Dunhill store near Union Square; it was a long shot, but maybe someone there would be able to identify its purchaser.

The piece of metal with the leather attached to one end could have been from a watchband; also the silver buckle. But buckles and chains went into so many accessories these days . . . long matches? Well, what else would you use to start a fire in a windswept lot? Ballpoint pen, dog bone paper clip chain? Junk. Gold cord? Same.

I yawned. Looked at Jessie the cat, who was eyeing me in hope of more food.

"Tomorrow, Miz Scarlett," I told her, "is another day."

Then I scooped her up and carried her to bed.

■ ■ ■ ■

FRIDAY, MARCH 9

■ ■ ■ ■

8:10 a.m.

Hy phoned me right before he boarded his plane home from Des Moines, sounding grim.

"Situation here's been resolved, and the one out there's still under wraps, but Gregor Deeds, the op I put in charge of the Hoffman case in my absence, reports we've received another series of those weird, taunting e-mails."

"Read them to me."

"I'd rather not; this isn't a secure line. How about I meet you at one o'clock in that parklet near our building? I'll bring hot dogs and Cokes."

"See you then."

9:41 a.m.

I'd decided to deliver the gold lighter to Richman Labs myself, knowing it would expedite my request to analyze the remains of its contents and identify any prints if I asked in person. I was just leaving there when Mick called.

"You all set for our evening with the Night Searchers?" he asked.

"I guess. But what if Givens shows up and recognizes me?"

"Jeez, I'd think you, of all people, would know how to disguise yourself."

"Of course I do, but the man's seen me up close and recently."

"It'll be dark. Givens might not even show, and if he does, you just slip into the shadows and abort your involvement."

"Sorry, I'm not tracking too well."

"Late night?"

"Late and bad. Dreams, you know."

"Yeah, I do."

We made arrangements for meeting that night, and then I touched base with Julia.

"Chad loves Italian food," she told me. "At lunchtime yesterday I followed him to a restaurant named Bella near his office building on Sacramento Street, where he ate for three hours: antipasto, scampi cocktail, soup, pasta, fish, roasted lamb, and a gooey, disgusting dessert. And wine, lots of wine."

"You were right there in the restaurant?"

"In a small booth across the aisle."

"Did he notice you?"

"Nope, he was too busy eating."

"What did you have?"

"Are you worried about my expense account?"

"No, I'm just curious."

"Minestrone, garlic bread, and a gooey, disgustingly wonderful dessert."

"No wine?"

"I was working a case . . . well, yeah, two glasses of Chianti. But during three hours of observing a pig, I felt entitled."

"Rightfully so. Where'd Kenyon go next?"

"Home to his house on Pacific Avenue. While he was at the restaurant, he didn't speak or have any other kind of contact with anybody except the waiter."

"Keep on him."

"If he goes out again tomorrow, can I eat whatever I want?"

"Eat anything you please, but go easy on the wine."

10:45 a.m.

Patrick Neilan, red-haired and ruddy-faced, was sitting in my office when I arrived.

"Done with the deadbeat dad," he said, "and Ted tells me you can use help on another case."

"Oh, yeah, can I ever." I plunked my briefcase down on my desk and myself in my chair.

"Surveillance?"

"On a client."

"Uh-oh."

"Name's Jay Givens." I explained the case and gave him a folder with the details and a photo of the subject that Mick had pulled off the Net. "Stay with him no matter where he goes, especially at night." I filled him in on the Night Searchers' activities.

"Right. I get it. What about the wife — this Camilla?"

"I'd like someone on her, but everybody else is tied up."

"You know, that woman you hired as a temp a few weeks ago — Erica Wilbur — strikes me as a person with a talent for our kind of work."

"Really?"

"She's jazzed about investigation, very detail-oriented, logical, and observant."

"And?"

"Okay, I'd like you to keep her around, so I could see more of her."

Romance and business. They seldom work, but sometimes they do. Witness Hy and me.

"Why don't you send her in and I'll talk with her?"

Erica Wilbur had come to us because of an ad we'd placed three weeks ago for someone to transfer our older case files to our central computer. She'd proved to be efficient and, though somewhat shy, fit well into the mix of personalities. When she entered my office, she nervously pushed a strand of her long dark brown hair behind her ear — something I'd seen her do before in times of stress. Probably she was afraid I was going to tell her that we no longer required her services.

I motioned for her to sit, and she did, pulling the hem of her shirt down as far as it would go — which wasn't much. The way she folded her hands and crossed her legs at the ankles reminded me of an anxious little girl at dancing school.

"Patrick tells me you're excited about investigative work," I said.

"Oh, yes." The edgy expression disappeared and her gold-flecked eyes shone. "I've been reading some of the files I scan. That is okay? I'm only reading them for my own information."

"It's okay as long as you don't discuss what you read with anyone outside the agency. How much information have you picked up about surveillances?"

"Quite a bit. Always take water and food and something to . . . pee in. Don't stare fixedly at any one point, but scan the scene. If in a car, park inconspicuously. Wear dark clothing, even in daylight, and have a couple of changes in case you need to go someplace where what you've got on isn't appropriate." She was ticking the items off on her fingers. I stopped her before she got to number five.

"How'd you like to run a trial surveillance?"

She asked eagerly, "When?"

"Right away." I pushed the file containing a photograph and information on Camilla Givens across to her. "I want to know where this woman goes and what she does twenty-four seven. If you see her with a man and spot Patrick in the vicinity, don't be surprised or acknowledge him. I've got him on the husband."

"I'll read it and be on my way in my trusty Ford Falcon."

Ford Falcon? As far as I knew, they hadn't been manufactured in this country since the sixties. I hoped Erica's was more trustworthy than Rae's now-defunct Rambler American — called the Ramblin' Wreck — had been.

1:00 p.m.

Hy and I met at the parklet next to the RI building exactly on time. He carried the promised bag of hot dogs and Cokes. I carried what files I thought were relevant to our conversation. We sat down on a secluded bench to eat.

"Parklets" are another recent phenomenon in the city — or perhaps they've always existed but have now been given a name. Little grassy and well-landscaped oases — often equipped with benches, tables, and chairs — tucked away from the general foot traffic, where people can eat their lunches, have quiet conversations, or simply contemplate their lives. Most are privately financed, as was this one by RI; others are the products of nonprofits; a few are maintained by the already-strapped coffers of the city. They add to San Francisco's old-world charm and sense of concern for the well-being of its citizens.

Hy pulled a sheaf of papers from his briefcase and handed them to me. There, in the familiar capital-letters format, were five messages:

DON'T WANT HIM BACK AS MUCH AS WE THOUGHT, DO YOU?

THOSE SECRETS HE'S HOLDING ONTO COULD
TEAR THIS COUNTRY APART.

THE PRICE IS GOING UP EVERY MINUTE YOU
HESITATE.

HE'S PISSED OFF AT YOU AND GETTING
READY TO TALK.

YOU BETTER CAPITULATE — OR HE DIES.

"They — or he — are getting more aggressive in his tone," I said. "Frustrated that there's been no publicity or definite response."

"So let's up his aggression and frustration. Those're two emotions that can lead to revealing actions."

"Dangerous actions too. We don't want any more out-of-control killings in this country."

"This guy's not dangerous. Not like that."

"How d'you know?"

"Believe me, McCone, for more years than I care to remember, I've sat across tables in interrogation rooms from guys like this. Give me a little time and I'll figure out how to lure him right into our arms."

"Okay. Now we need to talk more about the situation. I e-mailed you about those

128

conflicting reports from the family members. Which sounds the most genuine to you?"

"None, but there's a grain of truth in all of them."

"Let's start with the Global Policy Forum. I put Derek on it, and it turns out that it *is* going to be terminated. Leaving Hoffman out of a job and with minimal retirement and health benefits."

"And the violence that the one daughter talked about?"

"No hospital or emergency services reports. Doesn't go with the apathy his niece Suzy described to me."

"Jane Hoffman's take on things . . . ?"

"Doesn't count. She's either an expert liar or so far out in la-la land that I don't think she'll ever make her way back."

"Terrific family." Hy shook his head. "Crazy mom, crazy daughter, estranged daughter, and Suzy, who seems to be the only one of them who's halfway well wrapped."

"Or devious mom and daughters. Suzy's really the only one I trust — with reservations."

"Which are?"

"I sense she doesn't like any of the others, and as the favorite niece, Suzy has a great deal to gain if they fall out of favor with their parents."

"As I said, terrific family."

3:45 p.m.

Julia came into my office looking tipsy. She flopped into a chair, removed the abalone-shell combs from her hair, and let it fall.

"What a day!" she exclaimed, exhaling heartily.

I could smell her breath: red wine and garlic.

"Imbibed a bit again, huh?"

"A bit? No, a lot. That Chad Kenyon can really put his booze away. And eat? That man could gobble down a whole steer and then ask for an ox." She burped and clapped a hand over her mouth. "Sorry. I hooked up with him for lunch, and he practically forced me to keep pace with him."

"How'd you manage that? The hooking up, not the keeping pace."

"Wasn't difficult. He came out of his office building, went to Bella — same restaurant as last night. Same private booth. I asked the waiter for the booth across the aisle. Only this time I oogled him."

"Oogled?"

"Maybe it's pronounced *ogle.* Anyway, turns out he really is a sucker for Latina beauties — that's what he called me, a Latina beauty."

"And you called him?"

"Chad."

"Okay, while all this talk of your beauty was going on, did you manage to learn anything of relevance?"

She cast me an indignant look. "Yes, I recorded the conversation. It wasn't a situation where I could take notes, and I was afraid that with the wine, my mind —"

"I understand." I had been there a number of times myself. "Play the tape."

At first there was some talk about what Julia did for a living — she'd inherited a lot of money from her mother, who was a descendant of one of the original Spanish land-grant families, and didn't have to work, but she had once published a book of poetry and was thinking of setting up a gallery to aid unappreciated young artists. Then Chad talked about buying and selling things. ("Never hold on to anything longer than sixty days, that's my philosophy.")

Julia interjected, "Chad hates his brother Dick."

And apparently he did, for his voice went on and on about the number of their shared deals Dick had cost them by failing to make the right move at the right time. ("He's a loner. Doesn't want to negotiate. Just wants to go off to his cabin in Cazadero and sit in the woods.")

"Where the hell is Cazadero, anyway?" Julia had asked him.

"Sonoma County, the western hills."

"I've never been there."

"It's nowhere land. And Dick just sits in the woods. What kind of man does that?"

"What should he be doing?"

"Tending to business, dammit! We've got this building site, bought it two years ago and started the foundation for a high-rise. Then when he's supposed to go to get the other permits, he doesn't. He just hangs around in the woods. Says it gives him peace. I should get some peace sometime, maybe. But that ain't gonna happen in this life."

"So what's your next project?"

"We're leaving for Europe tomorrow — Amsterdam — if I can get him out of the woods."

"Going to buy Holland?"

A pause, then a chuckle. "Why not?"

Julia shut off the recorder. "The rest is mostly eating noises, and you don't want to hear *those.*"

"You bet I don't. So the Kenyons are pretty much out of the picture."

"Sorry I couldn't get anything significant."

"It was a blind lead. As you know, you get a lot of them in this business."

"Well, at least I got a couple of great meals."

5:10 p.m.

Mick said, "I'm not getting anyplace. There's some pretty sophisticated stuff blocking access to these sites."

"What're you looking at?"

"Van Hoffman's personal accounts. His company's. Even the flight service he uses."

"What about commercial airlines?"

"Doesn't fly them, according to his executive assistant."

"And how did you find that out?"

He did a good imitation of a villain's leer for me. "I met her for coffee. She's pretty, hot, and twenty-two."

"And you worked your magic."

"Um, sort of."

His tone was short, meaning it was an avenue he didn't care to pursue because it would lead straight to his relationship with Alison. I respected his silence; he'd tell me when he was ready.

"Let's go over our plans," he said. "Seven thirty, we're to meet in the Panhandle, under a cypress tree near Masonic and

Lyon. I think we ought to drive there separately; we might need two vehicles later."

"So then we follow the clues, and somebody wins the prize."

"That's about it. I know it doesn't sound all that exciting to you, given what you've been doing all these years, but I can see its appeal to people with basically nothing in their lives."

"Actually, it sounds pretty interesting."

"Unless there's danger involved that we don't know about."

"If there is, we'll deal with it."

He looked at his watch. "If we're to make it by seven thirty, that leaves just enough time for you to treat me to a home-cooked meal."

6:45 p.m.

The meal wasn't really home-cooked, but Stouffer's lasagna and a bagged green salad with cranberries and candied walnuts are always good. Hy wasn't home yet, so I covered the rest of the meal with foil and left it on the kitchen counter for him. Then I made a quick call to Camilla Givens, asking if we might get together — just she and I, and I emphasized it this time — for a talk in the morning.

134

"Have you found out anything?" she asked eagerly.

"Quite a bit."

"But why do you want to talk only with me?"

"Just as a time-saving measure. You and Jay have said he's very busy; so am I."

"I see." She agreed to ten thirty, and I noted it on my iPhone.

Next I went upstairs and changed into black jeans, walking shoes, a sweat shirt, and a pulldown knit hat. The only things about me that could be seen in the dark were my nose and chin, and I added a black scarf that could be wrapped around them.

When I came back down, Mick said, "You look like a cat burglar."

I surveyed his dark attire. The stocking cap he wore was ridiculous and sported a white ball at its tip. "Remove that white thing," I told him.

"It's Alison's skating hat, she'll kill me."

"I'll buy her a new one."

"Okay." He ripped it off and tossed it into the garbage can under the kitchen sink.

"Looking good now," I said.

We set out — me in my Mercedes and Mick on his Harley — for the Panhandle of Golden Gate Park, where the hunt was due to begin.

The Panhandle is a long, wide, grassy median strip between the main arteries from the bridge to Golden Gate Park. Cars sped by on the bordering Fell and Oak Streets. It had begun to sprinkle, and the pavement was wet; tires whooshed on it, and horns blared at the scenes of near collisions. It always amazes me how we San Franciscans can live with so much rain, yet drive in it so badly. Maybe it's the result of our fixating on our expectations: we believe that we are entitled to sunny days and starlit nights, even if we don't get a lot of either.

Mick had wedged the Harley into an illegal space and stuck a press pass he'd gotten from a friend at the *Chron* on its windshield. He swung off the bike and stood beside it, waiting for me. I ran down the sidewalk from a spot I'd located across the street. Together we sheltered under the trees. After a moment I whispered, "The Panhandle always seems small when you're driving by, trying to beat the lights, but it looks huge tonight."

"Darkness makes everything seem huge." In Mick's voice I caught the slight edginess that told me he was not quite afraid, but close to it.

We looked around and got our bearings.

136

Wind rattled the branches of the cypress trees above us, and rainwater dripped onto our heads. I shivered as cold droplets dribbled between my scarf and my collar.

"Shit," Mick said, "why would anybody want to play a game in this weather?"

"Maybe it's been canceled."

"No, I've got a feeling about the Searchers — the worse the scenario, the better."

As if their bearers had been cued, three flashlight beams bobbed on the other side of the greenbelt. We watched as they shone on a big juniper bush and someone scrabbled around inside it.

Mick grunted. "Not the place they told me to look."

"Where, then?"

"Over by that housing for the sprinkler controls."

"You go there and see what you can find; I'll keep an eye on these."

"I don't think we should split up."

"Nonsense. Just go. If our paths don't cross, I'll meet up with you later at the office."

The juniper branches were scratchy. I felt through them, found a plastic bag toward the bottom; within it, paper crackled.

I removed the paper, turned my flash on it, and read — in bold-faced font — Follow the five flashlights.

I looked around and saw the lights, bobbing a hundred yards or so away by Fell Street, the westbound artery that leads beside the Panhandle and through Golden Gate Park. I hurried toward them. The people — dressed in dark clothing — paused at the intersection with Masonic, then ran through the traffic like carefree children. In the light from streetlamps and cars, I could see well enough to tell that Givens wasn't among them.

I followed and pulled back onto the sidewalk in time to avoid being squashed under a Safeway delivery truck. The driver viewed me with horrified eyes through his side window; I tried to smile and waved him on.

Two blocks ahead, the people with the flashlights were turning right on Grove Street, a block I knew because a friend had once lived there. The dwellings were mostly multiple-unit, none of them over two or three stories. In the glow from the streetlights they looked white, although I remembered them as being painted in various pastels. The olive trees in brick planters on the sidewalk, which had been saplings a few years ago, had grown tall.

Mick was already there, waiting under a tree; I moved through the shadows and joined him. We watched the group of five mount the steps of a house in the middle of the block. One of them, a woman, went up to the bank of three mailboxes, extracted a manila envelope, and read its contents with the aid of a pencil flash. I moved closer.

7:59 p.m.
After a couple of minutes, the woman cleared her throat and said in a husky voice, "Kilkarzo, you're paired with Malanzky. Here's your first clue. Alinzsky, you go with Dizarsky. And hey, newbies, you been following us too long; come with me."

It took me a moment to realize that she was speaking toward where Mick and I were sheltering a few yards away. We came out from the shadows and hurried down to where they were now grouped on the sidewalk.

The woman who seemed to be their leader looked us up and down. "I'm Grizeldy. We gotta give you your Night Searchers names." Her brow knotted in thought. "Vaskazy? I've always been partial to the letter *V.*"

"The letter *Z* too, I suppose," I said.

"You got it." She was short, round-faced, with wisps of gray hair straying from under a knitted cap similar to mine. I couldn't tell much about the others, as the streetlight over our heads was out. "What d'you think?" she asked the group.

"Vaskazy," they answered in unison.

"And him." She motioned at Mick. "I've got that one picked out: Loverzboy."

"Why?" Mick asked.

"Because you're hot."

Even in the shadows, I could see him blush.

Grizeldy said, "What're each of you gonna contribute to the prize pool? First game, players give up something."

"The prize . . . oh, right," Mick said. "How about my Saint Christopher's medal?" He slipped it over his head, and I stared at it in amazement. Then I recognized it for what it was: an object from our property room.

"You?" Grizeldy said to me.

I'd forgotten the prize pool. I searched through the pocket of my jeans and came up with a coin from Finland that I kept there for good luck. "It's rare," I said as I handed it to Grizeldy.

She barely looked at it. "Okay, let's get on with it. Loverzboy, you go with Kilkarzo and Malanzky." She poked my arm and said, "This way." I followed her toward a rusted old orange Honda that I hoped wouldn't crap out on our journey to wherever. Before we got in, I got a good look at the license plate number and committed it to memory.

"First clue," Grizeldy said, "Lafayette Park."

Pacific Heights. Expensive neighborhood.

"And what do we do there?" I asked.

She gave a harsh laugh. "What d'you think? Scare small children? Kidnap rich people's lap dogs? We pick up another clue, dummy. Hopefully before any of those other clowns do."

Otherwise Grizeldy didn't have much to say, even though I tried to engage her in conversation. Instead she chain-smoked Marlboros until I needed to put my window down.

"Health nut, eh?" she said.

"Not really. I've just never smoked."

"Never?"

"Well, weed in college. But all it did was make me paranoid and stupid."

"So what *do* you do for kicks?"

"Drink and screw, and now I play Night Search."

That provoked a hearty laugh. "Hey, you're okay."

"You been doing this long?"

"Couple of years, more or less."

"And how long's the game been going on?"

"At least a decade. That's how long our founder's been in town."

"Who's that?"

"You don't need to know."

I decided it was time to back off on the questioning.

8:33 p.m.

Lafayette Park: a green and flowered respite with incredible views nestled in a neighborhood of elegant old apartment buildings and single-family homes. Tennis courts, picnic areas, acres of room for children and dogs to run. But eerie at night. I don't know why that should be; so far as I know, nothing truly horrible has ever happened there.

To me, encounters with hostile homeless people or deranged individuals aren't as intimidating as to the average citizen. But the park still felt dangerous to me at night.

Grizeldy double-parked the car on the Washington Street side of the park and ordered me to stay there. The last I saw of her bulky shape, she was climbing the grassy slope.

She returned some ten minutes later, breathing hard and coughing. "Why do they always hide the stuff in places that're hard to get to?" she asked.

"Who are 'they'?"

She shook her head, started the Honda — failing on the first try — and said, "Next stop, Alamo Square."

9:25 p.m.

Alamo Square: a pleasant park northeast of the Panhandle in a quiet residential area known as the Western Addition. Its greatest claim to fame is its view of the city's "painted ladies" — an impressive, beautifully maintained row of Victorian homes that are probably the most photographed of all the features of the city, except for the Golden Gate Bridge and Coit Tower. When we arrived there, Grizeldy again told me to wait. I took the time to go through her glove box.

Her name, or at least the name of the owner of the car, was Jill Kennedy. She lived on Twenty-Third Avenue in the Sunset district. I found no insurance cards, but what decent company would write a policy on a piece of junk like this?

I reached around behind the driver's side seat, found an assortment of crumpled papers. Parking tickets. I slipped a couple of them into the deep pocket of my jacket.

Just in time: Grizeldy returned, her breath rasping now. It took her a moment to get it under control. "Fuck!" she exclaimed.

"Now we're supposed to go all the way to Aquatic Park."

Not far from my house in the Marina.

"Do you want me to drive?" I asked.

"Why should you?"

"You sound . . . like you need to relax."

She took an inhaler from her pocket, breathed deeply. "It's just these goddamn allergies."

To me, her distress seemed more serious than mere allergies.

"Well, I don't mind driving."

"Maybe later." She took another hit off the inhaler. "You know, could be I'm just getting too damn old for this stuff."

"Then why do it?"

"Why do *you* want to do it?"

"The highs, I guess." I thought back to what Alison's psychologist friend had told me. "I've got a pretty shitty job — file this, call so-and-so — you know what I mean. But when I can go out like this, in the dark, where I know that fat, middle-aged boss of mine wouldn't dare venture . . . well, I guess it makes me feel powerful. So I can get through another nothing day."

"My reasons exactly. Here I am, a plain, little, ordinary woman. Living a plain, little, ordinary life. No family still living. No friends, except for the Night Searchers, and

I don't even know their real names. So I go out and I take risks and win a few prizes. But one of these nights, I may win the prize I really want."

"And that is?"

"You'll find out — when I win it. Okay, now I'm all right for driving to Aquatic Park."

10:21 p.m.

All the way across town I kept my eyes on her and her driving. She frequently shook her head as if to clear it and she switched lanes erratically and missed turns no matter how many times I reminded her. On Polk Street near North Point she smashed into the curb while trying to park in a large space. I grabbed the wheel, let the car slide into a more or less legal position, and removed and pocketed the keys.

Grizeldy — who I assumed was Jill Kennedy, the car's owner — was hugging the steering wheel and crying. "I can't do this any more tonight. You follow the clues, please. You win me my prize. I'll pay you, I promise." She thrust the envelope she'd retrieved into my hand.

"You need medical attention —"

"No, just need a little rest. Go down there, get the next clue. I think we're still ahead of them. Please! That prize is important to me."

I didn't want to leave her. She didn't look well, seemed to be having trouble breathing. Bad allergy attack, or something more serious?

Should I call 911? I knew Grizeldy wouldn't like that, but sometimes you have to act for another person's well-being in spite of their preferences. But San Francisco's medical emergency response time is horrendously long — as the budget for it is horrendously low.

And then I thought of Adah and Craig, who lived only a few blocks away. Both knew CPR better than I. Either could be there in minutes, if they were home. I called and luckily, they were. And willing to come immediately when I explained the situation.

While I waited, I kept a consoling hand on Grizeldy's shoulder; she was only semiconscious now. After a moment I turned on my flashlight and opened the envelope she had thrust at me; inside was a computer-generated note: The clue is under a loose curbstone near the first burned-out light on the Municipal Pier. Proceed!

Adah and Craig arrived quickly, he with a little bag he kept in his car for emergencies like this. Craig checked Grizeldy's vital signs, shook his head. "Doesn't look good. She needs oxygen, a defibrillator, God knows what else. And by the time emergency services get here, she'll probably be gone."

"We'll take her ourselves," Adah said. "And you" — she pointed at me — "go do what you have to."

10:47 p.m.

Terrific. The rain was lashing down again, the few lights on the pier were dimmed to faint oval globes, and I was supposed to go out there and root around before any of those other maniacs arrived.

The Maritime Museum building sits at the foot of Polk Street, facing a man-made lagoon that used to be called Black Point Cove. Originally a bathhouse built in 1936 by the WPA, the Moderne-style structure is now dedicated to the city's seafaring past. To the west the long, horseshoe-shaped Municipal Pier extends into the Bay's chill waters. Tonight, with the rain sprinkling and the wind gusting, the only people in the area were a few hardy souls who had braved the storm to visit the shops and restaurants of Ghirardelli Square, but even they were leaving now. The business lights of the former chocolate factory, which sits catercorner to the museum, were winking out, and the remainder were dimmed by the rain.

I had a friend who had once worked at the museum, so I knew about the steep driveway that would take me to the pier more quickly than the established route. As I walked, the ground was slick beneath my feet, my supposedly water-repellent parka soaked clear through. Once I was on the pier, it was hard to keep my footing. Clutching the side rail, I went as fast as I could to the first pole where the light was burned out, squatted, and studied the curb. It was in poor repair, with wide cracks in several places; one stone block was out of kilter.

I pushed the block aside and found a manila envelope. Looked around to make sure I wasn't being observed, then took the envelope to one of the functional light poles, shielding it from the rain before reading. It contained a small note card of heavy stock; I wasn't sure how much time I had, so I didn't bother to read the message, just photographed it with my cell phone. Then I replaced the card in the envelope and the envelope under the stone and went farther down the pier to where another one of the lights had burned out. Watched and waited.

As I did, I checked out the photo on my cell: "North, south, east, west: you know where the hiding's best," the bold lettering said. It was signed "The Night Searchers."

The message meant absolutely nothing to me. A Night Searcher insider's clue, it seemed.

After about five minutes a figure in a dark-colored parka — male, from his size and gait — came skidding down the slope tourists use and made for the pier. No one I knew, fortunately. He reached the first nonfunctional light pole, hunkered down, and began moving the stones. No — hurling them this way and that, the destructive bastard.

He apparently found the envelope, because he hurried off the pier and climbed back up the slope to the parking area at the end of Van Ness.

The rain was letting up again as I ran for where Grizeldy had parked the ancient car half a block away on Polk Street. As I started it up, I reflected that I was, in effect, stealing it. No, I corrected myself, moving it to a safer location at the owner's request — or the request she'd have made if she'd been conscious.

God, my powers of rationalization are strong!

Just as I drove to the main parking lot for the Municipal Pier, a dark-colored sedan — Audi? Volvo? — gunned past me. Its driver was male, possibly the Night Searcher in the dark-colored parka. I pulled a U-turn and went after him.

The other car skidded around the corner of Polk, made an erratic left turn on Bay Street, and began weaving in and out of traffic, heading, I thought, for the Embarcadero. But just before we came to the intersection with Columbus, the car shot around a stopped Muni bus, and as I tried to follow, the bus laboriously pulled away from the curb. By the time I cleared the intersection, stopping twice for pedestrians walking against the light, I'd lost the sedan.

Even in this inclement weather, the sidewalks were crowded and the gaudy lights from the North Beach clubs flashed through an incoming fog. Music thrummed loudly from various sources. A bicyclist — dark clothing, no helmet, no reflectors — nearly clipped me. Finally I pulled the Honda into an illegal space at the curb so I could think without also having to concentrate on driving. The sedan could have gone right, into the financial district, or straight toward the piers. Caught the freeway and headed east over the Bay Bridge or south toward the Peninsula. Or doubled back toward Marin and points north. Or . . .

The hell with it.

Grizeldy's heap made a horrible grinding sound as I eased it away from the curb. Then it shook violently, belched a hideous, oily cloud of smoke, and gave what sounded like a death rattle.

People ran — both away from and toward me. Horns began honking as traffic backed up behind me. Their drivers pulled by me when they could, a number of them shouting curses out their windows.

"Are you all right, miss?" An elderly pedestrian in formal clothing rapped on my window.

"Yes." I took his arm as he helped me from the car and sheltered me with his umbrella. "But this . . . this . . . *thing* . . . !" I kicked viciously at its tire.

A woman with the same type of umbrella, who might have been his wife, patted my arm and said, "There, there, dear."

A techie type — one of the three-piece-suiters whom I dislike on sight — remarked, "Serves you right for driving a piece of shit like that."

The older couple looked shocked. "Young man, mind your language," the woman said.

More horns were honking as the stopped traffic built up. "Move that damn car!" a man shouted.

"Me and my boyfriend'll help you push it

to the curb," a younger woman in a parka and jeans said.

"Okay. Thanks a lot."

Along with two other volunteers we got the Honda out of harm's way. In the morning I'd arrange to have it towed to the garage I patronized and have it fixed at my own expense; I felt guilty that I'd probably done something to make it break down and, besides, I sensed it was one of the few things Grizeldy owned. Both the older couple and the young woman and her boyfriend offered me a ride home, but I declined, saying I could manage on my own.

My phone trilled and I moved into an unoccupied doorway to answer it. Adah.

"We're at the hospital. Had some trouble getting Jill admitted, since we had no insurance info."

"Naturally. Assurance of payment above all else. What's her condition?"

"They won't tell me. I'm not a relative."

"Oh, for Christ's sake! Give me the charge nurse."

When the man came on the line, I said, "This is Sharon Kennedy. The woman my friends brought in is my sister, Jill Kennedy. I'm staying with her at her home on Twenty-Third Avenue. Can you tell me her condition, please?"

"I'm sorry, but if you'll come in and present your identification —"

Fuck that! "Is Amanda Lui on duty tonight?" She was the nurse who had aided me through the early days of locked-in syndrome.

"Why, yes. She's right here."

"Let me talk to her."

Lui came on the line, and I said, "It's Sharon McCone."

"Shar! How are you?"

"I'm fine, but a friend of mine isn't. She was brought in there a little while ago by two of my employees."

"Ah. The unidentified woman who had the severe asthma attack."

"Yes. Her name's Jill Kennedy. What's her condition?"

"Critical. She's in and out of consciousness."

"Making any sense?"

"Some. You want your associates to keep notes on what she says?"

"If Nurse Ratched will permit it."

Lui's voice hardened. "She'll permit it — or else."

"Great. May I speak with Adah? That's the female half of my team."

Adah came on the line. "What's happening with you?"

"Too much to go into; my cell's losing power. Will you come pick me up?" I gave her my location. "And take me to the hospital so I can see the patient?"

"I'll be there asap."

■ ■ ■ ■

SATURDAY,
MARCH 10

■ ■ ■ ■

1:25 a.m.

Jill Kennedy was in an oxygen tent, with tubes snaking around her and IVs piercing her pale skin. I wouldn't have recognized her as the vibrant woman lining up her Night Searchers only hours before.

Amanda Lui came up behind me. A petite woman with her black hair tucked into a net, she looked frail, but I knew from experience how much strength was stored in her small body. "Oxygen deprivation's caused some brain damage — how much, it's hard to tell. And her heart's very weak."

"You're saying she's not going to pull through."

"Probably not. She's still tossing around and mumbling from time to time. If you wait, maybe she'll tell you what she wants to communicate."

As if on cue, Kennedy moved her head. "Prize," she whispered.

Lui gave me a little shove. "It's okay to talk to her."

"Jill . . . Grizeldy. What prize?" I asked.

"Got to . . . get to . . . it."

"What prize?"

"Big one. Mine. Used to . . . be mine. Till I donated it."

"When?"

"Got to get it . . ."

Lui said, "She's losing consciousness again. I don't think that she's going to be able to talk any more."

"I'd better get out of here. I'm making things worse."

"I'll call her doctor but, yes, you'd better go. If she says anything else, I'll let you know."

2:20 a.m.

Hy had arrived home while I was at the hospital, and we were having a nightcap — or maybe I should call it a morning-cap — in front of the fireplace in our bedroom when Mick finally called.

"Those Night Searchers," he said, "they are one strange crew."

"Tell me about it."

"I've got their aliases — including Jay Givens's and Van Hoffman's — down and enough other information to run checks on their real identities. The one I was paired with is a guy calls himself Darezarro. He joined us later. Big, way overweight. From some of the tats and prison jargon he tossed around I think he might be an ex-con."

"What did you and your ex-con do?"

"Followed clues all over the city. The Tenderloin, Richmond district, Duboce Triangle, Sunset Reservoir. But then Darezarro was drinking vodka and decided to call it quits."

I explained to Mick what had happened with Jill Kennedy.

"Poor woman," he said. "To tell the truth, she didn't look so good."

"Probably something that's been coming on for a long time." I didn't want to talk about it any more tonight. "Okay, thanks for the report," I said. "Sleep in today."

"Till when — six o'clock?"

"Six thirty. You're young — four hours should do it."

"You're a tyrant."

"And you're an esne."

"A *what*?"

"Look it up in the dictionary."

Esne, of course, meant slave. That should broaden Mick's vocabulary significantly.

7:06 a.m.

The alarm went off. Alex jumped off my feet and Jessie jumped onto my head. Another morning had begun, and I was due at the office at eight. Beside me, Hy moaned sleepily.

"Sorry," I said, "have to get up now."

He moaned again and looked at where his watch lay on the bedside table. "And I have to leave for Miami in three hours."

"Miami? You didn't tell me —"

"My mind wasn't on Miami last night." He reached for me, but I eluded him and went to turn on the shower. When I came back, he was propped on his pillows, arms crossed behind his head, frowning.

"What?" I asked.

"I suppose, as you often say, we're leading the lives we've chosen. Being free, doing what we love to do."

"I suppose."

"Then tell me why I feel those lives have chosen us."

"And you tell me why I feel those lives are *leading* us."

11:19 a.m.

I looked at my watch and realized that I'd missed my ten thirty meeting with Camilla Givens. Damn. That wasn't like me at all.

160

I called her number and, surprisingly, she was gracious. "Why don't you come right away? I've got a luncheon appointment at one o'clock, but we'll still have plenty of time to talk."

I agreed and rushed out of the office, ignoring pleas from employees who wanted something from me.

The Givens condo looked better by day than by night, with the hideous Hawaiian-print curtains drawn open and daylight filtering in through the pale beige sheers. Even the cow chair, where Camilla insisted I sit, didn't seem quite so ugly. Still prickly, of course.

Camilla served coffee, then sat on the sofa, lighting a cigarette. "I hope you have good news, Ms. McCone," she said.

"Interesting questions, anyway. But before I start — how are you?"

"Doing well."

"Have you had any more of those odd experiences?"

"Not a one. I'm hoping they've stopped for good."

"I hope so too." I took the evidence bags from my briefcase and placed them on the table between us. Opened one and held up the metal piece by the sections of cloth attached. "Have you ever seen this before?"

She shook her head. "Where's the rest of it?"

"I wish I knew."

"It's been burned, hasn't it?"

"Yes. Now this bag" — I held up the one containing the small links of silver chain — "are its contents familiar to you?"

A blink. She stared at it, running her tongue over her upper lip. "It looks like part of a bracelet, the kind you have in high school that you're supposed to put charms on. I had one, but I don't remember what happened to it."

"What about this?" I showed her the gold lighter.

". . . I used to have one like that, but its insides got fucked up and I lost it someplace."

"Where?"

"I don't know. If I did, I would've gone back and found it, wouldn't I?"

"Have you been out on any of your nighttime walks since I last saw you?"

"God, no. I was taking those walks because I was trying to give up smoking and couldn't sleep, but I've gotten so I'm afraid to go out after dark without my husband along. Which means I don't go out much, because he's never around. And I'm smoking more than ever." She crushed out her half-smoked cigarette in an ashtray already filled with butts.

"Do you ask him where he goes?"

"I've given up on that. All I get are vague answers: 'Meeting that ran overtime,' 'Client dinner,' 'Business trip out of town.' "

"What about his involvement with the Night Searchers?"

"Who are they?"

"He's never mentioned them?"

"No."

I didn't want to get into explanations, so I asked, "I know this is an invasive question, but how would you describe the state of your marriage?"

She considered, lighting another cigarette. "Well, it's not awful. Jay doesn't abuse me or anything like that. When we go out, he's very attentive. We don't have sex often, but I understand that's the case with most overworked couples. Not that I'm overworked, but . . . I don't know . . . I'm tired a lot of the time."

"Any interests in common?"

"We watch a lot of movies." She gestured at a wall of videotapes and DVDs. "I cook. I've taken classes at the Culinary Institute, and he appreciates my gourmet meals."

"Sports?"

"No, neither of us is athletic. Jay doesn't

even play golf."

"Mutual friends?"

"Couples — ones that he does business with the husband."

"Opera? Ballet? Concerts? Museums and art galleries?"

A headshake to each question.

"You have many women friends?"

"Not really; all my old friends are scattered. I have one friend here in the city whom I'm close to. Anita Glynn."

The name had appeared in Mick's files.

Camilla added, "But she's busy with her career — civil engineering — so we don't get to spend as much time together as we'd like. I guess I'm pretty much alone. Jay tells me I should get out, volunteer, do something useful. But I feel pretty useless."

"That's probably temporary."

"I hope so. It's scary, feeling so separated from everyone and everything."

"Well, if you ever want to talk again — privately, like this — you know where to find me."

"Thank you, Sharon. You don't know how much it means to me."

1:13 p.m.
Mick arrived at my office, clutching a stack of papers and a big tote bag that smelled of

barbecue. Now that the city has outlawed plastic shopping bags and requires a ten-cent fee for paper ones, most people have started carrying whatever they happen to have around the house or can locate in the thrift shops. Of course, the issue of how sanitary frequently used totes are was immediately raised — but how can you regulate the frequency with which residents wash their bags?

Frankly, this city dwells on the small stuff entirely too much for my taste. When you've got people without food, shelter, or medical care, maybe they need those plastic and paper bags to carry their meager possessions. Why not focus instead on supplying them with the necessities? Recently I'd been reading about numerous costly studies the city was commissioning on the homeless problem. Researchers and statisticians receiving taxpayers' dollars that could have been used to fund more soup kitchens, mental health programs, shelters, and — that all-important factor — educational opportunities.

I motioned to the papers Mick was dumping onto my desk. "What're those?" I asked.

"My research." He divided them into two piles, and pushed one my way.

"And you did this research when?"

"From when I talked with you on the phone until half an hour ago. That's why I don't look so spiffy."

He didn't look even close to spiffy: unshaven, eye bags from lack of sleep, wrinkled clothing, and a bad case of rumpled hair. But, bless him, he'd stayed up working all night . . .

"You're terrific, you know?" I said.

"Don't get sentimental. Just read this stuff, and then we'll talk."

For an hour I read, making notes on a legal pad that was smeared with sauce from the baby back ribs I was eating. At some point during this period of deep concentration, Mick went out and returned with another round of Cokes. I swilled and gobbled and read on.

"So," I finally said, squaring the pages in front of me, "these Night Searchers really don't know each other. Still, I keep thinking there might be some sort of link between Van Hoffman and Jay Givens."

"Me too. Is there any further word on Hoffman?"

"As of the time I left the house this morning, no."

"Check with Hy, would you?"

"He's on his flight to Miami by now. I'll call my local contact, Gregor Deeds."

Deeds, Hy had told me, was a former CIA operative who had gotten tired of working in a political climate and turned to the private sector. Last year he'd accepted a job with RI, bought a house in the East Bay community of Albany, and moved his wife and two young children west.

Deeds was in his office and fully informed on the Hoffman case. "No, nothing new on Hoffman," he said.

"This situation Hy's involved in — is it heating up?"

"Think so. It's been exacerbated by events in Central America. But don't worry, Ms. McCone. He filled me in on all the details of what you're handling, and we're holding up our end of the case too. Anything you need, just call."

"Thanks. By the way, I'm Sharon to you."

"Gregor to you."

After I clicked off the phone, I turned to Mick, who was staring at Mr. T. as if the plant contained some profound secret of the universe.

"You still with me?" I asked.

"Uh, sure."

"There's nothing further on Hoffman."

"Damn! So all we have is this tenuous connection among him, the Night Searchers, and the Givens couple."

167

"You know," I said, "I'm beginning to think that these Night Searchers aren't at all the benign game-players they claim to be. Let's talk them over, starting with the aliases Givens and Hoffman use."

"Givens's is Zoneout. Hoffman's is — was — Yazoosky."

"Silly names. Why can't they use normal ones?"

"Well, it's a silly game, if you think about it."

"What about Zero, the woman they claim is their founder? Your report said she was the most difficult to identify and track down."

He nodded. "Marlene Daniels. Spotty history, even in childhood. Born in a Fort Wayne, Indiana, home for unwed mothers. Given up for adoption, but no takers."

"Is she Caucasian?"

"Yes."

"Odd, there's always been a big demand for Caucasian infants. Something wrong with her?"

He made a note. "I'll find out. Anyway, she kicked around from foster home to foster home, ran away from the last when she was sixteen. Next trace that I could find of her was in Berkeley, eight years later."

"A student?"

"Nope. Street person. Hooked up with one Al Zeronsky. A college dropout. Zeronsky's kind of interesting: was right on track in the PhD program in philosophy, left without any explanation. An all-A student in high school in San Bernardino, expected to go far. Now he works for a carpet installer and his old lady's a clerk at Kinko's. No criminal record on either. They're married, have no kids."

"And both have boring jobs. Good candidates for the Night Searchers."

"Next, Grizeldy. Any word on her condition?"

I looked at my watch. "Amanda Lui, the nurse I know there, said she'd call if anything changed. Tell me about Grizeldy — I mean Jill."

"Uneventful life. Has lived in the city since her birth. Her mother left her a little row house on Twenty-Third Avenue. Attended public schools, went to Heald College for secretarial training, has worked for the same insurance company where they placed her twenty-some years ago. Unmarried, no children."

"Anything about her, besides having held the same job forever, that uniquely qualifies her for the group?"

Mick smiled the way he always does when

he has an interesting tidbit to report. "Well, there *was* the alien abduction."

"What?"

"Uh-huh. Welcome to *The X-Files*. Her father disappeared when she was eleven, and she claimed she'd seen him abducted by extraterrestrials. Was a big story in the media for a while. What *wasn't* a big story is that he was found ten years later, living with his fourth wife in Oregon. Since he hadn't bothered to divorce the other three, he went to prison for serial bigamy and died there. But Grizeldy — Jill — sticks by the abduction story."

"God. Another perfect candidate."

Mick nodded. "Now we come to Malanzky. He's a fan of the old *Perry Mason* TV movies. They're all he watches — over and over. He identifies with the character Ken Malansky, who appeared in most of the later releases."

"Ken Malansky — the assistant who was always getting hit on the head?"

"Right. Our Malanzky is Paul DeSoto, a used-car salesman from Daly City. Married, three kids. His job, I suppose, gives him the perfect excuse to be out late at night. He grew up on the Peninsula and went to San Mateo High. Undistinguished record, and no indication of higher education."

"I wonder if the wife and kids also watch Perry?"

"They could do worse. And last, Alinzsky. True name Timothy Mantis. Rabble-rouser without a cause. Was a great admirer of Saul Alinsky, the community organizer."

"The guy who threatened to stage a 'fart-out' at a performance of the Rochester Philharmonic, and a 'piss-in' at O'Hare Airport?"

"Shar, why do you always remember the worst aspects of people's lives?"

"They don't seem all that bad to me. Alinsky's methods were unorthodox, but he energized and influenced a lot of people."

"You mean you'd have gone to a 'fart-out'?"

"Sure. Or to a 'piss-in' if I was pissed off enough."

Mick gave me the look he reserves for when he doesn't know whether I'm kidding or not.

"Who else?" I asked.

"They're the core members. Givens and Hoffman played frequently, but not every game. And then there're others who play the game occasionally, but I don't know enough to identify them yet."

"Okay, let's get back to this Timothy Mantis. What does he do?"

"He prays."

"Praying Mantis? Oh, God, no puns!"

"No, really. His thing is praying for death to all capitalists. He turns up in public places, mainly the Civic Center. Wearing a long white robe. With a big black beard, bare feet, and long toe- and fingernails painted purple. People describe him as a horror."

"Well, I'm not sure that's worse than showing your often unattractive naked body parts in public." A while back the city had been hit with a nudist craze — finally outlawed by the board of supervisors — centering in the predominantly gay Castro district. The one glimpse I'd had of the Naked Guys, as the press had dubbed them, had not been a pretty sight, but they were benign; they just wanted to — so to speak — hang out, not pray for anybody's death.

"There's a lot more in this file," Mick said after a moment. "Dates, specifics. I'll get on to the occasional players tomorrow."

"And I'll take the file home, go over it in detail tonight."

He looked at me as if there was something he wanted to ask. Then he nodded. "You have any questions, I'll be at the new place on Potrero, helping Alison unpack."

4:40 p.m.

I was about to leave the office when Kendra Williams, our receptionist, brought back an envelope addressed to me from Richman Labs; it was labeled "Personal & Confidential." I opened it and read the report with increasing interest.

The gold lighter I'd brought them was an ordinary Dunhill that had been on the market for five years; as I'd suspected, its stippled surface could not take fingerprints. Its contents, however, were more dangerous than butane, the usual lighter fluid. That was present, but had been mixed with two reactants to form a powerful substance that can do serious harm to the nervous system. One or two inhalations of the altered gas can cause a person to experience hysteria, paranoia, temporary memory loss, psychosis, or death by asphyxia.

A note from Lonnie at the lab said she'd be happy to give me a more detailed explanation if I'd drop by sometime. Tomorrow I'd call her.

5:47 p.m.

Home, lovely as it was, wasn't where I wanted to be, so I drove out to Rae and Ricky's house above China Beach in the Sea Cliff district and invited myself for cocktails.

173

Rae looked happy to see me, even though she'd obviously been working, in the blue velour sweats she favored, her red curls loose around her shoulders.

"Nice surprise," she said. "Want a martini? Ricky just mixed up a batch."

Normally I avoid mixed drinks because they befuddle my thought processes, but tonight I was already befuddled, so what the hell?

"Sure. Where *is* Ricky?"

"Down running on the beach."

"In this rain?"

"He's got a six-state concert tour coming up, and he thinks he's gotten fat."

"Ricky, fat?" I laughed.

"Middle-age love handles," she called from the kitchen. "But he can't be all that worried — it's a short beach."

I followed her and took chilled glasses from the fridge. "Where's Mrs. Wellcome?"

Phyllis Wellcome was their housekeeper — a stern-looking, gray-haired woman of indeterminate age whose appearance masked a lively sense of humor and even more lively curiosity. She was prone to eavesdropping and then rendering opinions — often right on — about the people she'd listened to. In fact, she had once told me she could be "persuaded" to help out my

174

agency "when domestic matters" were involved.

Rae poured the martinis. "She's staying at the Ritz-Carlton tonight."

"What?" It was one of the top luxury hotels in the city.

"Yeah. It's her birthday, and she always treats herself to something nice. This time it seemed different, though — I think she's got a beau."

"Oh?"

"I just happened to peek into her room and saw her packing some pretty racy underwear and a red gossamer nightie."

"My God, that woman gives us all hope."

We went into the living room, and I sank onto the sofa before the pit fireplace, my back to the threatening gray skies over the sea. "So what's going on with you?" I asked.

"Things're good. New book's due out in May."

Rae had set out years ago to write a "shop-and-fuck" novel — her favorite genre. Instead she'd penned — or computered — a gem of a romantic thriller, and others had followed.

"Trouble is," she added with a frown, "I don't know what to do for the next one."

"Why don't you take off on my current case?" I explained about the Night Searchers to her, and after a few sentences she picked up one of her ever-present pads and a pen and started making notes.

The back door slammed and Ricky came down the hall, dripping water and wiping his hair with his sweat shirt.

"Hi, Chubs," I said.

He tossed the shirt at me and I caught it. "Hi, Trouble." It had been his nickname for me ever since I'd ended up living in their guest room after a vengeful client burned down my house in Glen Park.

He added, "When the rain started to pour down for real, I should've known I'd find you up here."

"What am I — a harbinger of bad times to come?"

" 'Harbinger of bad times to come,' " he quoted. "A good song title, but how many people know what 'harbinger' means?"

"Do you?"

"Yup. Want the dictionary definition?"

"Spare me."

"No, really," he insisted, "a harbinger is an omen, a sign, or a person whose appearance predicts . . . ah, fuck the harbingers," he said, "I've got to take a shower."

Rae laughed. "Sometimes he amazes me," she said as she handed me my drink.

"Why?"

"Well, when I met him, I thought he was gorgeous and sexy and a great entertainer, but I supposed he'd be dumb as a post. So many of them are."

"And now?"

"He's gorgeous and sexy and a great entertainer — and smarter than most people I know."

"Wow," I said, "using the word 'harbinger' will probably get him laid tonight."

Rae flushed and looked into her drink. "He never even graduated from high school. He was on the road with his first band when he was sixteen."

"I know." Then I changed the subject. "So this Night Searcher case," I said, "you want in on it? Might inspire you."

She looked thoughtful, nibbling at a fingernail. "It might at that."

"It'd be nice to work together again."

"Would."

"You in?"

"I'm in."

We shook on it.

9:23 p.m.

The opportunity came sooner than either of us expected, via a phone call from Mick while we were on our second martini.

"Something's going on with the Night

177

Searchers tonight," he said. "There's this one fairly regular player, Jim Norman, that I've gotten to know because of our mutual interest in Harleys. He hinted at it, asked if I was going along."

"And you're not."

"No, neither is Jim. But he's a born eavesdropper and found out it'll end up on the waterfront, near those piers that're gonna be replaced by the Warriors' stadium."

The Golden State Warriors, the area's major-league basketball team.

"And that's all he could tell you?"

"It's all he knows."

"Thank him for me. And tell him to keep eavesdropping."

So now here Rae and I were, in the recessed doorway of an office building near the intersection of Brannan and Beale Streets, not far from the approach to the Bay Bridge overpass and Piers 30 and 32. Traffic thundered overhead and a few cars swished by on the wet pavement, but otherwise the largely industrial area was deserted. The rain, thank God, had slowed to a drizzle.

"Shades of yesterday," Rae said.

She was, I knew, referring to when the agency had been located in Pier 24 1/2.

"Do you miss it?" she added.

"Yes and no."

"Me too. Shar, are we getting soft in our old age?"

"Old age?" I muffled my laughter. "You're younger than I am!"

"I know. But sometimes I feel like I'm getting too fond of this plushy life I lead with Ricky. And you — look at the Mercedes Hy bought you. To say nothing of your new house."

"We haven't abandoned our work and sat around eating potato chips all day."

"Or swilling martinis — well, not usually, and tonight's have worn off by now."

"So stop indulging in unwarranted guilt."

"Yes, ma'am."

We waited a while longer. The foghorns outside the Gate lowed like discontented cattle, and the rain came down harder. Street activity in the vicinity was minimal.

I was equipped with the agency's night scope, which allowed me to see over five hundred times more than the naked human eye perceives in darkness; Rae had an infrared camera with nearly the same capabilities and a highly sensitive recorder.

With the advent of the Warriors' state-of-the-art, multipurpose recreation and entertainment facility, this was another place along the waterfront that was about to change radically. And not a bad thing, since the two piers were crumbling, rat-infested, and mainly used for parking. But to me — the old nostalgic — the radical change was still somewhat sad.

"Jesus," Rae muttered, "can you *believe* him?"

"Who?"

"Ricky. Pouting because I decided to come with you. He knows this is work — we discussed my book. It's not as if he can't order a pizza."

"Ricky's kind of a high-maintenance guy, as if you didn't know."

"Yeah. But he can't expect to rule my life."

"Trouble in paradise?"

"Maybe, but not the kind you think. He hasn't been unfaithful; I doubt he's looked at another woman since he met me. He's been totally supportive of my new career. But he travels all over the place and when he's here, he wants me here with him."

"Isn't that flattering?"

"I suppose so, but sometimes it conflicts with what I need to do. So he pouts. Does Hy pout?"

I smiled, trying to imagine such an expression on my husband's rough-hewn face.

"I thought not," she said.

"Mick pouts," I said, by way of consolation.

"That's probably why he's lost so many women."

"Maybe it's a Savage family trait."

"Well, if it is, Ricky's going to get the trait kicked out of him."

Minutes passed. Then Rae tugged my arm and whispered, "Over there."

Flashlights were bobbing along the opposite sidewalk from the northwest. We drew back into the shelter of the building's entry, and I focused the night scope on them. They were bundled in rain gear; I couldn't recognize any of them as they passed by us, beams focused on the ground. All I could tell was that three people were moving in concert — men, I thought, from their size. They wore dark clothing, and I couldn't make out their faces. They kept going toward the Embarcadero.

"The Searchers?" Rae whispered.

"Maybe." I fine-tuned the scope. Stepped out of our shelter to train it on the group. I recognized Kilkarzo and Malanzky, but couldn't make out the features of the man in the middle.

After they'd gone maybe twenty-five yards, I took the scope off and motioned to Rae that we should shadow them.

They crossed the wide Bay-side boulevard and turned south. A stylish new streetcar rumbled past, interior lights shining through the rain. Rae and I sprinted across and stopped in the shelter of a pier's arched mouth to let the group get farther away. Then we moved after them, staying in the shadows, maintaining the same distance as they passed a few piers protected by gated and locked chain link fences. Finally they turned toward one where the arched mouth yawned open.

The pier — 38 — was one of the more derelict on this part of the waterfront: inside its open shell sat a jumble of forklifts and barrels and broken-down crates, barely illuminated by security lamps mounted on the overhead beams. The wind blew rain through it, whistled as it exited over the Bay. It was one of the most lonesome urban places I'd ever seen.

The threesome didn't go into the pier, however, but passed around it. I slipped ahead of Rae to the building's corner and peeked around. They were huddled at a waist-high seawall that guarded the shoreline. The slap of the waves was loud, the odors of creosote and brine pungent. Their clothing billowed in the sharp wind off the Bay, obscuring their companion. Behind me, I heard Rae's camera softly clicking.

The unidentified man shifted his stance, and when I had a glimpse of his profile, astonishment caused me to break stride.

The man was Van Hoffman.

I started to run.

For a moment the trio stood at the seawall, looking like a prayer circle. I could hear voices, but not words. Then their energy shifted perceptibly. Suddenly Hoffman hurtled over the top of the wall and into the water. There was a splash and spray shot up, splattering the remaining two.

"Hey!" I yelled and heard Rae shout something behind me.

The two men at the seawall froze for an instant, startled. Then they fled, going in different directions.

I reached the seawall and peered over. Hoffman was splashing around ineffectually, as if he couldn't swim or the shock of the icy water had taken his breath away.

I toed off my shoes, dumped my night scope and parka, and, without thinking, boosted myself on top of the wall and plunged into the Bay.

Cold! Jesus Christ, how cold!

I surfaced, coughing and gagging on the dirty water, pawing at my eyes to clear my vision. Hoffman was about ten feet away.

Already my hands and feet were numbed by the cold. Aware of the danger of hypothermia, I swam over to him, struggling to keep afloat. Got an arm around his neck in a lifesaving hold and started towing him toward the supports of the pier. Up above I heard Rae shouting for me.

When I reached the pier, I slung an elbow across a lower beam and hung on to the man till Rae had dragged him up and then returned to help me.

On the pier I knelt and threw up what seemed like a quart of bilious water. The Bay has us fooled: it looks beautiful, but it tastes not only of salt but of oil, creosote, and rotted fish — as well as other noxious substances.

Rae wrapped her coat around me while she called 911, and got me swaddled like an infant.

I asked her, "Is he alive?"

"You got to him in time. Van Hoffman, isn't he?"

"Yeah." I took Rae's hand and struggled to my feet. Water sluiced off me as if I were a wet sponge somebody was wringing out. Hoffman lay on his side a few feet away, where Rae had dragged him. I stumbled over to him. His eyes were open and roaming about: conscious and alert.

I knelt to take a close look at him. "Help is on the way," I told him.

"Who're you?"

"Sharon McCone, an RI associate."

"Oh." He squeezed his eyes shut, miming unconsciousness.

I put my lips to his ear and said loudly, "Who were those men you were with?"

He kept his eyes shut, but I could see rapid movement behind the lids.

"Who *were* they?" I shouted.

His eyes opened. "Kidnappers."

"Your kidnappers brought you down here, pushed you into the Bay?"

"No. Jumped to get away from them."

"Who are they?"

"Don't know."

"Why did they bring you here?"

A cough. "Don't know. Kill me, maybe."

"Where were you being held the past few days?"

"Not now," he said in a rasping voice. "Can't talk any more." He rolled his head back and forth on the cold concrete. In the distance I heard the wail of a siren.

"The EMTs are coming. They'll make you comfortable."

"Want to go home." His head flopped to the right and he appeared to pass out.

So why did I think he was faking it? And

why did I sense he'd been lying?

I flat-out refused to go to the hospital. I'd seen enough of such places to last my lifetime. I wanted to go home; I wanted Hy; I wanted warmth and clarity and sanity . . . yeah. Instead I got to sit bundled in a blanket in the back seat of a police car while they loaded Hoffman into an ambulance. Then I got to sit there some more while the uniforms questioned Rae and me. Finally I sneezed a couple of times and they provided me with a heavier blanket and tissues.

Plainclothes inspectors arrived. I didn't know any of them; my rapport with the SFPD had become strained over the past few years, since I'd lured Adah away from them and my old friend and lover, Greg Marcus, had retired.

I sneezed again — two, three, four times — and Rae took my lead and sneezed too. They moved us to their car and turned up the heat. I repeated my account of what had happened twice; it was easy because it was true. My husband's company, RI, had an executive protection arrangement with the Global Policy Forum. They had been informed by Jane Hoffman that her husband was missing. Since Mr. Ripinsky had a crisis

186

in South America to attend to, he had subcontracted the Hoffman case to me. Now Hoffman had been found and the rest of the story could be gotten from him. My operative, Ms. Kelleher, had photos of what had happened. End of my part.

Of course, it wasn't the whole truth: I kept all mention of the Givenses, the vacant lot, strange rites, and infant sacrifices out of it. I didn't want to spend the night locked up in the psych ward.

I asked if I could be taken back to my car, then couldn't remember where I'd parked it, then realized we'd come here in Rae's. Rae was still being questioned by the cops. We'd be able to leave together sooner or later.

When I got out of the back seat, after promising to give a formal statement about the incident, one of the cops demanded their blankets back. I stood shivering and looking around for Rae among the few remaining people on the scene. When she finally appeared, she draped me in my thick down parka and handed me my shoes. The cops drove us to where she'd left her car, and I must have gone to sleep, because the next thing I remember is Ricky leaning in the doorway of Rae's and his guest room.

"Trouble," he said, "we're gonna have to start charging you rent."

■ ■ ■ ■

SUNDAY, MARCH 11

■ ■ ■ ■

6:10 a.m.

I woke with a start, oriented myself — not here in Rae and Ricky's guest room again! — and slipped out of bed. Rae had taken my sodden clothes away, and I had only the too-big bathrobe from the guest room closet, but my house wasn't all that far away and nobody would notice what I was wearing in the car.

The car . . .

I went downstairs, looked out the kitchen window. There was the Mercedes, parked exactly where I'd left it in the driveway yesterday. Nobody else was up; I supposed Mrs. Wellcome was still off on her birthday adventure.

The coffeepot, set on a timer, was brewing. Either Rae or Ricky had anticipated my early departure. I sat down to wait till it was finished. Then I drank a cup, found my car keys in my purse, and left for home.

The cats were starving. They wound around my legs and made frantic sounds, and dug in as soon as I'd put their chow down. Hy still wasn't back, and they'd gotten into the food I'd left out for him and eaten it all.

"You guys are pigs," I said.

They didn't even look up.

"Yeah, you two — pigs."

Jessie gave me a "So what?" expression. Alex kept eating.

I grabbed my cell and called Mick, who sounded tired and cross when he answered. "Rae filled me in on what happened last night. I'll get the film from the infrared and have it developed." There was a pounding sound in the background. "Hold on." Voices muttered, and then he returned to the phone. "Cops," he said, "looking for you."

"Me? Why?"

"Didn't say, but they asked where you were living. They'd already been to the agency; I suspect the Avila Street address hasn't made it into their databases yet."

"Why the hell are they after me?"

"You haven't seen the early TV news?"

"You know I don't watch news on the television."

"Van Hoffman claimed to hospital staff and then to the police that he was kidnapped and held in an unknown location by you and other people who wanted him to give up confidential information and, after he did, you took him down to the Bay and threw him in. Then you dived in and tried to drown him. Fortunately an unknown Good Samaritan rescued him. He says he can't give any reason for your actions."

"What? *I* was the Good Samaritan! *I* saved the bastard's life, and *this* is how he repays me?"

"Shar, take it easy. RI operatives are already all over him, demanding he tell the truth. He's not responsive to them now . . . but when Hy gets back —"

My blood was at full boil now. "Why would he tell such an outrageous lie about someone who's trying to protect him? What is he covering up?"

"I don't know, but you'd better concentrate on protecting yourself now. It's only a matter of time till the cops find out about the Avila Street address."

"I think I'd better clear out of here."

"And go where?"

"I don't know. I'll be in touch."

I punched the Off button, fuming, then speed-dialed Glenn Solomon.

I took a perverse pleasure in rousting the

attorney from his bed at an unsuitable hour for a Sunday. He moaned and groaned and made various unlawyerly noises before he came fully alert.

"What have you gotten yourself into now, my friend?" he asked.

I told him about Van Hoffman's inexplicable assertions that I'd extracted matters of national security before trying to drown him.

"Did you?"

"Glenn!"

"First question I ask my clients is whether or not they're guilty, and I don't discriminate as to who the client is."

"Well, I didn't. I tried to save his life, and this is the thanks I get. I should've let him drown."

"Ungrateful bastard." He was silent for a moment. "Let me check to see if anybody's taking this ridiculous story seriously. In the meantime, don't answer the door or pick up your house phone. I imagine you're calling on a secure line?"

"Very few people know the number."

"Smart girl." By way of apology he added, "At my age, any female under sixty is a girl."

He got back to me in fifteen minutes. "Looks like a lot more than the local authorities want to talk with you," he said grimly.

"Who, exactly?"

"The FBI. Homeland Security too. I'd advise you to cooperate with them."

"Oh, yeah. And watch them laugh before they toss my ass into a cell. I think I should keep a low profile for a while."

"Well, *I* think you should cooperate fully. There'll be an arrest warrant out on you if you don't."

"Not until I find out what's behind these lies."

"God, you're a stubborn woman." He sighed heavily. "Years ago I learned not to contradict your instincts. Where will you go? To that ranch up in Mono County or the seaside place?"

"Neither. I can't continue to investigate from a distance. The Savage household, for all their security, is too obvious. As is RI's suite. But RI recently bought another safe house. The deed of trust probably hasn't even been recorded yet, and it's as unlikely a place as anyone would ever imagine." I tried not to think of the cockroaches and whatever else resided there. "So far it's empty."

"This is not a course of action I would recommend."

"I'm not asking for a recommendation. Only a little help."

"You don't trust my judgment."

"I trust it — ninety-eight percent of the time."

"You and my wife. How did I get mixed up with such ornery women?"

"Just lucky, I guess."

"Okay, that safe house is where you'll go. Contrary to my upright image in the community I am not above a little chicanery in the interests of justice."

9:47 a.m.

As I packed the bare necessities at home, I kept trying to find answers to Hoffman's behavior. Why had he lied about my trying to drown him in the Bay? What could he possibly expect to gain? How did he even know about my investigation?

I was so damned pissed at this turn of events that I caught myself grumbling aloud as I grabbed one of my big, soft pillows, a new set of sheets, and a down comforter and shoved them down the stairwell. In the kitchen I packed food — mainly sandwich makings and chips and cheese puffs — and, of course, wine and a corkscrew.

The cats — Adah or Craig would take care of them. I made the necessary call — going out of town for a while.

10:32 a.m.

When Glenn picked me up it was a relief to get out of the house. The phone had been ringing nonstop: media people leaving messages, Mick calling me to announce that "government guys in suits" with search warrants were swarming all over our offices. I knew it was only a matter of time before they turned up at Avila Street.

After we'd talked at the old motel at the beach the other day, Hy had given me a master key that would trip no alarms. Now I wondered why he'd thought I might need it. My husband — always one step ahead of me.

I entered through the lobby door and asked Glenn to set my stuff on the reception desk. "You'd better go now," I told him. "That town car of yours is sure to attract attention the longer it stays outside."

After he'd gone I moved through the motel, checking it out thoroughly. The inner corridors smelled bad: mildew, musty carpet, and just plain dirt. The walls were a muddy brown that matched the worn carpeting. There were only twelve units, all of them barely habitable: crazily cracked mirrors; bureaus with scrapes and scratches and

197

missing drawers; stains on the curtains and bare mattresses that I didn't want to examine.

Home sweet home.

I went back to the manager's suite and tried to make it seem comfortable. Nothing short of demolition and rebuilding could do that. Then I went to take a shower and found the water was turned off.

In frustration I grabbed my cell and tried to call Hy. The damned thing's battery was dead — and in my haste that morning, I had forgotten to pack its charger. All the motel's phones were disconnected, as was the electricity.

Well, what had I expected? Cable TV and room service?

For a moment I considered going out to a public phone, then discarded the idea. These days, with the proliferation of cellular technology, they were too few and far between. I'd be exposing myself unnecessarily.

Misery. Total misery. I went straight for the cheese puffs and wine. Together they would get me through — for a while.

1:14 p.m.

I hadn't slept well in a long time, so I rolled myself up in the fluffy comforter and tried to nap. Instead I lay awake listening to every sound: the roiling waves on the beach across the highway; the revving of car engines in nearby parking lots; drunks quarreling on the street. Curiously, no one came near the red-headboard motel; perhaps word had spread that the new owner was armed and dangerous.

Except he wasn't here. And I was — unarmed and uneasy.

5:08 p.m.
I had to get out of there or go crazy. By mid-afternoon I was thinking seriously — if melodramatically — about disguises.

My most successful one had been when I'd cut my hair to shoulder length. After nearly a lifetime of having a long, waist-length mane, I'd felt naked, but even some of my relatives wouldn't have recognized me. Now I was happy with my hair and didn't want to cut it any shorter, so my options were limited to altering speech, style of clothing, gait, and makeup. Or — of course! Injuries.

When I was in rehab after my locked-in episode, I'd noticed that others — even if they were visitors to patients with injuries more severe than mine — looked away from me as I breezed through the hallways in my motorized wheelchair and, later, on my crutches. They never looked at my face, only at whatever device was aiding me at the time. While I didn't have the wheelchair any more, Adah had the crutches, which I'd loaned her after she had a skiing accident a couple of years before. A fake cast and sling protecting one arm would further distract. Or a few bandages would change the configuration of my face, and no one but Hy or members of my immediate family would recognize me.

I thought the plan over more thoroughly. Were the crutches and sling necessary? No — too cumbersome and confining. Facial bandages were the way to go. Such a disguise would allow me to go about my investigation without being recognized and taken into custody by agents of any of the organizations looking for a person in possession of national security secrets.

Glenn would have advised strongly against my plan; the last thing he'd said to me was, "Stay put." But I knew Craig and Adah would help me out. Trouble was, how to get hold of either of them now that the phones were disconnected and I couldn't have charged my cell even if I'd had the device? Again I considered chancing my safety by looking for a pay phone. Again I decided against it.

Then I remembered another device — the one Hy had removed from the phone jack in the end room where we'd talked the other day. He'd said it enabled a direct connection to RI's panel of listeners, who monitored what was going on in the safe houses all over the world. If all the devices in this building were linked, the removal of one would black out every room. I didn't recall either of us returning it to the jack.

Down the musty corridor I went. The room where Hy and I had been was at the end of this wing; fortunately for me, its door had been left open a crack. My memory had been accurate: the device Hy had removed from the jack still lay on the little table.

I plugged it in. Said, "Is anybody there?"

"Who's that?" a man's voice asked.

"Who are you?"

"Your name first. You're trespassing on private property."

"It happens to belong to me — community property."

A note of relief infused the man's next words. "Ms. McCone, it's Steve Burry. The feds're looking for you and sucking around our offices because they know Van Hoffman was an RI client."

"They're sucking around my offices too."

"Are you all right?"

"I'm fine, Steve. Has Hy called in?"

"Not recently. We've been trying to contact him, but he's on a hush-hush job and incommunicado."

"Keep trying. He needs to know what's been going down." I detailed the situation and added, "I'd appreciate it if you'd notify Gregor Deeds too. And there are some other things you can do for me. Keep monitoring this building — it's fully live now."

"You staying there?"

"For a while."

"Should we post a guard?"

I considered. "No, that might attract attention. And I'm probably the only person who's stayed here in years."

"What else can we do?" Burry asked.

"I need some things that a couple of my operatives can provide." I gave him Adah and Craig's numbers. "My three-fifty-seven Magnum; it's in the office safe, and they have the combination. My laptop — it'll have to be charged to the max, since there's no electricity here; a cell phone that's also fully charged; and a stack of files that're on the desk in my home office. A high-powered flashlight. And clothes from my agency's prop room. Stuff I'd rather die than wear; Adah Joslyn will know what. Bandages and adhesive tape, the bigger the better."

"You been hurt, Ms. McCone?"

"No, I'm fine. I'm just . . . not going to be me for a few days."

Burry, who was used to intrigue, merely said, "Okay. I'll get on with this. And I'll keep the mikes in that place monitored."

5:43 p.m.

At the tap on the motel room door, I peered out through a slit in the curtains and saw a tall, powerful-looking man with deep ebony skin and close-cropped black hair that was receding from his high forehead. Dressed in jeans, a leather jacket, and a 49ers sweat shirt, he could've been a linebacker rather than a security specialist.

"Gregor Deeds, Ms. McCone," he said softly. I opened the door and he slipped in, arms full of bags and bundles, and looked around.

"Oh, shit!" he exclaimed.

"Yeah. RI's gonna have to do some major work on this place before they start stashing deposed sheiks and candidates for the Witness Protection Program here."

He deposited his burdens on the bed. "Well, nobody would suspect you'd stoop this low, so I guess you're safe. Anything else you need?"

"Yes — the agency's van, parked in an inconspicuous place. Reports on surveillances I've assigned to my operatives Patrick and Erica. Anything further that my nephew Mick's got on . . . well, anything."

"Van's already here, stashed in an inconspicuous place in the alley. It'll fit right in in this neighborhood, but won't be seen from the street or surrounding buildings."

The van was a ten-year-old Dodge Ram, with dings and dents to attest to its rough past. Its paint was white except for where it revealed an undercoat of robin's-egg blue, and on its doors you could see where the sign for Sparky's Hot Dogs had been painted over. We hadn't done anything about its appearance, but inside the hood was a powerful new engine and behind the front seat was a sophisticated surveillance system. No one ever gave the van a second look, but it had taken many looks at bad things that were going down.

"How're you going to get back?" I asked.

He grinned. "You ever heard of the bus?"

Oh, yes I had — during the time when I was restricted from driving because of my injuries.

"Are you going to be okay here?" Deeds asked. "Shouldn't we do something about getting the water and power on?"

"Water and power department trucks would be too conspicuous. Besides, I'm beginning to settle into this place. I've named it Cockroach Haven."

6:08 p.m.
After Deeds left, I called Steve Burry on my new disposable cell and gave him the number, asked him to circulate it. No, still no contact with Hy, he told me. Deeds had said he'd now be busy trying to find out if there was more of a connection between Jay Givens and Van Hoffman than we already had.

I pawed through the assortment of clothing from the prop room, deciding on tonight's costume. Not much was appropriate for night work, except for a bulky navy-blue sweater jacket so big that its sleeves covered my hands and its hem hung down to midcalf. The nicest touch, I thought, was a gaping hole in one elbow. With it I'd wear the black jeans and T that I'd put on at home this morning.

Next I experimented with bandages: one suggesting a cut over my left eyebrow looked good; below it I placed another along my jawline. I left the makeup for later.

The light was fading fast outside the salt-rimmed, filthy windows. I pulled the curtains till they overlapped, closed the door to the bath, and turned on the Maglite torch Deeds had brought. It was powerful, and I was afraid it might be seen even with the dark curtains closed, so I took it into the closet and read Erica's and Patrick's reports on their surveillances of the Givenses.

Camilla had done nothing on Friday except check her mailbox. At seven her husband had arrived and at eight they'd gone out for dinner at Rose Pistola and then returned home. On Saturday Camilla had shopped. All day, from leaving her house at ten to returning at four thirty. She had visited Saks, Abercrombie and Fitch, Bloomingdale's, West Coast Leather, Max Mara, Cole Haan, and Tiffany's. She'd emerged from the stores with big, medium, and little bags — every time with a smile on her face. At lunchtime she'd met a woman at a tearoom on Post Street; the photo Erica had taken through its windows made me wrinkle my nose. Little tables for two, with pink-and-blue-flowered chairs tied in back with a big pink bow and matching table-cloths and napkins. Quiches and other little treats too delicate to recognize from the photographs printed on the display menu posted in the window.

The description of the woman with Camilla matched that of her best friend, Anita Glynn. Camilla, Erica's report said, didn't seem like a troubled woman. She'd proudly shown off the contents of some of her smaller bags to her companion. And after they parted, she went to where she'd parked her car in the garage under Union Square. She deposited her packages in the trunk and then shopped some more. So far as Erica could tell, the Givenses had stayed home Saturday night.

Patrick's report on Camilla's husband differed in a few details. On Friday Jay had gone to his office and stayed in at the lunch hour; at half past noon, a delivery person from a nearby sandwich shop had taken an order to the firm. Twenty dollars had gotten him to reveal that one of the sandwiches was for the boss: something called the Dictator. What was in it? Patrick hadn't been able to resist asking. Roasted pork, hot chilies, salsa, American cheese, and sauerkraut. All Patrick could assume was that the sandwich was a tribute to both Fidel Castro and Adolf Hitler. Which didn't say a lot about Jay Givens's taste.

After he'd left his office at six thirty Friday evening, Givens had gone home and later taken his wife out to dinner. But the next morning, a half hour after Camilla left on her shopping spree, Jay went directly to an apartment building on Balboa Street near Sixteenth Avenue in the Richmond district. The building had ten units, and most of the mailboxes were unmarked. Patrick remained on surveillance across the street all night; Givens finally emerged at noon on Sunday and went home. Patrick was having Derek do a property search for the apartment house.

Julia hadn't had any further contact with either of the Kenyons; Chad was either away on business or shacked up with one of his many women friends. Dick was probably still sitting in the woods.

9:37 p.m.
Mick's call brought bad news: Jill Kennedy, aka Grizeldy, had died of cardiac arrest fifteen minutes earlier.

I felt a stab of regret, thought about her words when I asked her why she was a Night Searcher: *Here I am, a plain, little, ordinary woman. Living a plain, little, ordinary life. No family still living. No friends, except for the Night Searchers, and I don't even know their real names. So I go out and I take risks and win a few prizes. But one of these nights, I may win the prize I really want . . .*

No more prizes for Grizeldy. Not ever.

"Shar?" Mick said. "You there?"

"Uh-huh. Just feeling sorry for Jill, is all. Anything else?"

"I'm trying to get a handle on the peripheral members of the NSes. And track down this Zero woman. What're you doing tonight?"

"Oh, rereading files on the case. Waiting for phone calls. Staying safe."

"You sure you're safe out there? From what Gregor told me a while ago, it's kind of a Bates Motel."

"Don't worry. I've made a deal with the cockroaches to protect me."

"Your safety isn't a joke, Shar."

"And it isn't a problem, kiddo."

"Don't call me kiddo!"

I laughed and broke the connection.

11:04 p.m.

Just as certain questions nag at you until you're compelled to find their answers, certain places draw you because you know something's there that you've overlooked.

The big question I had was: were the Givenses, the Hoffmans, the Kenyons, the Night Searchers, and that vacant lot on Saturn Street all connected, and if so, in what way? So the place that had drawn me out of Cockroach Haven tonight was, of course, the lot.

Saturn Street was bleak and ugly, even in the darkness. As I turned right into it, I heard what I thought was a scream and then saw a dark-coated figure suddenly dart out of the shadows by the fence. Headlights from a fast-approaching car illuminated the running figure, but the person didn't stop, just dashed blindly into the street. Tires squealed as the driver swerved, not quite in time to avoid clipping the runner, who sprawled into the street. The driver regained control, then gunned the engine without slowing down. The car, a low-slung sports job, nearly sideswiped the van as it roared past. I twisted the wheel just in time.

Cursing, I braked to a fast stop, got out, and ran to the figure in the street. It was a woman, apparently not badly hurt, trying to struggle up onto hands and knees — and furious.

"Goddamn that son-of-a-bitch driver! He's one of them, he's got to be!"

Camilla Givens. I recognized her first by her voice, then by her jasmine perfume. Her face, when I finally saw it under the hood of her coat, was contorted with a mixture of fear and rage.

I leaned down toward her. "It's Sharon McCone, Camilla."

"I don't care if you're Jesus Christ! Help me!"

"Tell me where you're hurt."

"Everyplace."

"That's not an answer. Shoulder? Arm? Leg?"

"It hurts everyplace. Inside and out, all the time."

"Where, specifically?"

"My mind, my heart, my soul — if I have one."

She was overdramatizing her accident — and she knew I was aware of it. "Oh, God," she said. "Just pick me up and take me home."

I helped her up, and we walked toward the van. She was still trying to make more of her injuries than they really were, but gave it up when we were halfway there. Physically, she seemed nothing more than shaken up and maybe bruised. Once I got her seated in the van, I said, "I'll be right back," and ran to peer through the fence into the vacant lot.

No one was down there. The excavation was dark and silent. Then, as I was about to turn and walk away, something caught my eye — a red glow, as if from embers of a dying fire.

I could climb down and investigate, but

Camilla was spooked and I was afraid she'd slip out of my car and run off, searching for more weird happenings. Reluctantly I returned, found her slumped against the passenger's side door, crying softly.

I reached into my jacket pocket for my recorder. "Why on earth did you come back here, Camilla? I heard you scream. Tell me what happened."

What she told me — some of it sounding like previous tales — would be transcribed an hour later by Ted, who had been sleeping and growled at me for form's sake, but came into the office anyway.

C: . . . got this anonymous phone call telling me to come to this . . . horrible place.

S: Did you recognize the voice?

C: No, it was weird, distorted . . . scared me.

S: Then why did you go?

C: I needed to know. Something's going on, something bad, like all this other stuff that's been happening to me.

S: So you came here and . . . ?

C: And I looked down through the fence, and there were four or five of them.

S: Men? Women?

C: I don't know. They had on those damned hoods. But I could see what they were doing. [Sob.] They had a fire going under this big black cast-iron pot like my mama used to make stew in, and they were boiling something 'cause I saw the steam coming up.

S: What were they boiling?

C: Well, an infant, of course.

S: How do you know?

C: . . . Because . . . it's what they *do.* [More sobs.]

S: Okay, so that's when you ran?

C: No, I screamed and one of them looked up and saw me. The one with the sword.

S: Sword?

C: Yes, a sword! He saw me and waved it at me, and I screamed again and ran. After that . . . I don't remember.

S: Don't you remember the sports car that grazed you?

C: No. Wait . . . yes. Asshole driver!

S: Where's Jay tonight?

C: Jay's out, he's always out.

S: Out with the Night Searchers?

C: Who?

S: The Night Searchers. You must know about them.

C: I've never heard of them.

S: Was Jay there tonight? In the pit?

C: No.

S: Was Van Hoffman there?

C: . . . Who?

S: Van Hoffman. Your husband's fellow Night Searcher.

C: I don't know anything about any Van Hoffman or Night Searchers. Who are they?

S: I thought you could tell me.

C: I wish I could.

The problem now was what to do with her. She clearly was afraid of her husband and refused to go home ("If Jay has come back I don't want him to see me this way. It'll just be added to the list of his complaints against me").

This presented an ethical dilemma: Camilla was my client, but so was Jay; they'd both signed my contract. Should I favor one over the other?

Yes, my gut instinct told me. Camilla was afraid of her husband, and after the things I'd found out, I didn't trust him either.

She'd be too easy for Jay to find if I checked her into a hotel. I couldn't see exposing her to the squalor of Cockroach Haven. Or dumping her on any of my friends. The suite at RI was fine as far as security went, but I didn't trust her not to do something stupid. I needed a professional to look after her.

Gregor Deeds at RI came to mind.

■ ■ ■ ■

MONDAY, MARCH 12

■ ■ ■ ■

I felt comfortable turning Camilla over to Gregor Deeds.

Apparently he didn't inspire the same confidence in her. She shrank back as I made introductions and he held out his hand to shake hers.

Racial prejudice? God knew there was enough of that going around, but it didn't seem to fit with what I sensed of the woman's character. Maybe, given her situation, she was simply nervous about being put in the hands of a stranger.

Deeds ignored her rudeness, shrugged out of his jacket, and looked around the RI hospitality suite. "Man, these people in trouble live high. Huge-screen TV, gourmet kitchen, bet there's even a Jacuzzi tub in the bathroom."

"In both of them," I said.

"Oh, right, you'd know. You and the old

219

Rip stayed here for a while recently."

His reference to "the old Rip" reassured me further. It was a nickname only Hy's most trusted operatives called him.

As Deeds moved about the suite, commenting on its luxuriousness, I understood that he was searching for anything that might be a bug or a potential hazard. After a while he wandered back to where Camilla stood and asked, "You like movies?"

"Some, as long as they're not too violent."

"Well, we've got our choice of just about anything ever recorded on DVD. You like popcorn? With lots of butter?"

"Yes."

"The kitchen's loaded with stuff like that, and there's a state-of-the-art popper. And there's soda and beer and wine. Guess what we're gonna be doing while we ride out this little bump in your life."

As Gregor talked, I watched Camilla relax: at first her rigid fists; then her tensed shoulders; and finally her face.

"May I pick the first movie?" she asked.

"You can pick 'em all, darlin'."

I said I needed to go, but Camilla was too interested in the shelves of DVDs to give me more than a perfunctory wave. Deeds followed me to the door and stepped out behind me into the hallway.

"How on earth did you effect that transformation I just witnessed?" I whispered.

He shrugged. "It's what I do, bringing calm to troubled people. My daddy was a preacher, and he always wanted me to follow him into the church. Let's just say circumstances took me in a different direction. I'll tell you about it sometime, but right now I've got to figure out how that fancy popcorn popper works."

We said good night, and after some hesitation I took the elevator down two stories to my office. Wasn't likely that the guys in suits would be hanging around at this hour, but I entered by a door only the cleaning staff used and made sure it was locked behind me. It had been an exhausting day, and the sofa, a thick, woven throw, and the oversize pillow I kept in the prop room seemed like a little chunk of heaven. Still, I removed my .357 from my bag and placed it next to the pillow. Then, with regret I loaded the gun.

The previous year I'd declared myself through with weapons, after a case reminded me what a horrendous blight on modern society they are. My then-client — a staunch anti-gun proponent — had made me think seriously about the role firearms play in our lives. Ironically, at the conclusion of that case, I'd saved myself and those working with me by wounding and apprehending a murderer.

Since then I'd been seriously conflicted about the positive uses and disastrous abuses of firepower. The horrific killings at Sandy Hook Elementary School in Connecticut, as well as many others, muddied my thinking. I still visited the firing range and kept my weapons — the second being a .38 police Special — in good shape. I reminded myself that they were not weapons of war like the assault guns the shooter in Connecticut had used on those helpless children and faculty. But once serious doubt about something you've always taken for granted creeps into your psyche, it's a damned hard thing to dismiss.

4:06 a.m.

I awoke with a start, fingers groping for my Magnum, then realized the sounds that had awakened me were the voices of the cleaning staff at the far end of the hallway. They were chattering away in a mixture of Spanish, Filipino, Chinese, and other languages and dialects that have always sounded musical to me.

God, what if in my disoriented state I'd grabbed the .357 and leaped through the door, training it on them? Elisa, Jo, Lee,

Natalia, and Maria — not to mention the two new women — would have fled in a panic, and either quit their jobs or complained to the custodial supervisor. The owner's wife, as they thought of me, would be considered a head case. Not good for them to find me here. It was back to Cockroach Haven.

9:32 a.m.
Nothing from any of my operatives, nothing from Hy or anyone else at RI, nothing from Glenn. Had I dropped into a shabby, red-headboard alternate universe?

Well, that would be a fine kettle of carp, as my adoptive mother — who is prone to malapropisms — would say.

A tap on the door.

"Shar? You in there?" Rae. I went to the door, opened it enough so she could squeeze through. She looked like I did — another homeless woman seeking shelter.

"You shouldn't have taken the chance —" I began.

"No sweat. And I borrowed the new op's car — what's her name?"

"Erica Wilbur."

"Right. She's really nice, but the car's a piece of shit — like the Ramblin' Wreck. I brought food," she added. "Gregor Deeds

223

from RI called the office while I was there going over the report on the case. He asked me to make sure you didn't starve."

"What'd you bring?" I looked greedily at the bags she had set on the table.

"Go on, find out."

Deli sandwiches — big ones. Potato chips — salt and vinegar, my favorite. Freshly packaged Italian blend salad. Wine. Of course wine! And — oh my God — peach, cookies and cream, and Sinful Vanilla ice cream.

Rae had even thought to bring paper plates, plastic forks, and spoons. We dug in.

"How come Gregor Deeds sent you, instead of coming himself?" I asked between mouthfuls.

"He's busy on the Hoffman case." She grinned. "Besides, I think he was embarrassed to be alone in a motel room with the boss's wife."

"For God's sake, why?"

"I think he's got a crush on you."

"That's ridiculous. I'm years older than him. I've got crow's-feet, and I dye my hair."

"No telling about individual tastes. In second grade I had a terrible letch for Bobby Stravinsky, who was a sixth-grade hall monitor. You know, the guys who told you not to run or push each other."

"You had a *letch* for him?"

"Well, from an adult perspective, that's what it seems like. God knows why, given those buckteeth of his. And then there was Leo Burnell — I lured him into kissing me at a fourth-grade party and he never looked at me again. I guess I wasn't such a good kisser in those days. But I learned fast; practice makes perfect. And then there's Ricky —"

"I don't think he's in the same category with Bobby or Leo."

"Well, no. Or Jimmy or Matt or Charley or Miguel or —"

"Stop!" I knew enough about her checkered past not to want to hear any more.

"And then there was Willie."

"Spare me." Willie Whelan had been a receiver of stolen property who later cleaned up his act and became a legitimate businessman — owner of a company that specialized in cut-rate diamond jewelry for young lovers. He even performed his own outrageous TV commercials to hawk his wares on the off-brand late-night channels.

He hadn't given Rae a diamond, however, and later had been enticed to New York City, where he'd become a leading player as a villainous millionaire on a — then — top-rated soap opera. Rae and I had shared a bottle of champagne on the day the network announced it was canceling the show. But leave it to Willie: he now had his own prime-time cable show, titled *Reprobate.* From the few times I'd viewed it, I'd decided he'd convinced the scriptwriters to tell his life story in a highly fictionalized fashion.

In spite of myself, I couldn't help asking, "Willie still doing *Reprobate*?"

"Nope. He's become a TV chef, but that won't last. All he does is drop the food on the floor or set it on fire."

A Julia Child in the making.

"Also, he swigs some terrible jug wine."

His success was secured — at least in some parts of the country.

"Back to Gregor Deeds," I said. "You don't even work for RI, so why'd he send you?"

"I was the only one who answered the phone at the agency when he called to ask what you like to eat."

"Only you? Where were the others?"

"Out working on this case, I hope."

"What about Ted? What does he think? He and I have been together since day one. He's seen a lot of things go down, and his memory doesn't let go of the slightest detail."

"My bad. I didn't ask him his opinion.

But I will."

"Ask Kendra too."

"Why? Oh, of course, receptionists see and hear more things than most people."

"Right," I said. "I sense connections here, and I don't have an inkling of what they are."

"How long ago did all this weird stuff with Camilla Givens start?"

"Nearly three months now."

"There's got to have been a trigger."

"You mean something unusual that happened in her life back then?"

"Hers, or somebody else who's connected with her."

We rehashed the case for a while, scribbling on legal pads, entering data into our electronic devices, running searches — but came to no conclusion. Hoffman's obvious lies puzzled both of us. I sensed two parallel stories: the one that was supposed to have happened, and the one that ultimately had. But the details of both remained vague.

Belatedly I remembered I'd forgotten about asking Mick or Derek to try to identify Pamela, Hoffman's girlfriend. We tried calling both Suzy and Melinda to find out if they knew the woman's last name, but neither was available.

Finally Rae left and I continued perusing

Mick's files, pulling out the one on Marlene Daniels — aka Zero — the leader of the Night Searchers.

His notes read: *Marlene Daniels. Spotty history, even in childhood. Born in a Fort Wayne, Indiana, home for unwed mothers. Given up for adoption, but no takers. Caucasian. Odd, there's always been a big demand for Caucasian infants. Something wrong with her? Kicked around from foster home to foster home, ran away from the last when she was sixteen. Next trace of her — Berkeley, eight years later. Street person. Hooked up with Al Zeronsky, dropout from the graduate philosophy program, & they moved to North Beach. That address no longer theirs. A listing for Zeronsky, A., at an address on Bay Street. Nothing for Marlene Daniels or Zeronsky or Zero in the Greater Bay Area.*

I called the number for A. Zeronsky. After five rings a sleepy, half-drunken male voice answered. "Marlene?" he said in response to my question. "That ugly bitch? She left me two, three years ago . . ."

"She's now calling herself Zero."

"Zero? Must've shortened my name, just like she shortened my dick."

"Do you know where she lives now?"

"Yeah, I got an address in the Excelsior district somewhere. A buddy keeps me informed. I like to know where my enemies are."

"May I have it?"

"You gonna cause her trouble?"

I hesitated, gauging what he wanted to hear. "Probably."

"Hang on, let me get it."

1:20 p.m.

After Rae left, I contemplated going after Zero, but decided to put it off until after dark. The element of surprise is always greater at night — and surprise is one of the tools of my trade. So what to do till then?

I tried to read, but no matter which book I chose, it couldn't hold my attention. Even meditation, which I'd recently started practicing at the urging of my friend Piper, didn't do the trick. Finally I bundled up and went for a long walk at the Ocean Beach seawall. It was a gray day with crisp offshore winds, the water pale green and foamy. The kind of a day that makes for loneliness and regret. Even though I didn't particularly regret anything at the moment, I felt it gnawing at me, and soon I was mentally searching for past regrets to indulge in.

This has to stop, I told myself. *I've got too*

much time on my hands.

I made a right turn then and spotted a family going into the zoo. Aha! Soon I was laughing at the antics of our newest baby giraffe.

9:47 p.m.

The Excelsior district was pretty rough territory and hopped up even on a Monday night. Lowriders cruised on Mission Street; gang members with attitudes gathered on street corners, trading insults and lobbing empty beer cans and liquor bottles back and forth. Drunks wandered into traffic, prostitutes trolled the sidewalks, and numerous people proclaimed their insane views in loud voices.

The district isn't the seediest in the city, but it directly borders the very worst area: Visitacion Valley/Bayview/Hunter's Point. Lots of gang activity spills over, and a statistically suspicious number of Excelsior fires had recently burned decrepit but well-insured homes to the ground. I'd driven here in the agency's van; it fit right in with the territory.

I spotted the address Al Zeronsky had given me and began looking for a parking place. Good luck. Even if I'd found one, the heavy traffic would have made it impossible to stop and parallel-park. Slow traffic too. People called out from cars to others on the sidewalks and stopped to talk. Jaywalkers abounded. I had to look out for an unusual amount of people with walkers, canes, and crutches who had difficulty in the cross-walks. I went around the block three times. Finally, when I turned onto Mission, I saw two adjacent spaces opening up at once.

In front of me, a beer delivery truck — what was it doing here at this hour? — put on its flashers and stopped dead, leaving no room to squeeze by.

I put down my window and yelled, "Hey, move that! You're blocking traffic."

The man who'd come around to open the rear doors raised his hands in helplessness. "Sorry, lady. Emergency supplies."

10:17 p.m.
When I finally got to Zero's address, after walking three long blocks from a mostly il-legal space and putting up with obscene calls and whistles from drunken males and females, I found it was a unit off a long third-story gallery in one of those concrete-and-steel buildings that always make me think of prisons — minus the bars and guards. No light showed behind the lowered blinds. Asleep or out somewhere.

Still I rang the bell and, when I figured out it didn't work, pounded on the door. Pounded again, long and hard enough that the door to the next apartment jerked open and a tall black woman in a pink quilted robe popped out.

"You lookin' for Marlene?" she asked.

"Yes, I am."

"She's gone."

"Gone? When? Where?"

"For good, I guess. Piled her stuff into a little U-Haul van and took off yesterday. I dunno where. Frankly, I won't miss her coming and going in the late hours. Kept wakin' me up when I'm needin' my sleep."

I nodded sympathetically. "And now I've done the same. I apologize. Did you know Marlene well?"

"Uh-uh. That woman kept strictly to herself."

"She have a lot of visitors? Loud parties?"

"Not too many visitors. No parties. She's kind of . . . well, disfigured. Funny caved-in face, and her eyes and lips don't match on either side. Back of her head's flattened too."

"What caused that? An accident?"

"Nope. She told me she's been like that since she was born. Some botched delivery, I guess."

No wonder she hadn't been adopted.

232

Most people don't want disfigured babies, no matter what intelligence or emotion might be behind the mangled façade.

"So that's why she didn't have any friends," the woman added. "I tried to be, but she wasn't having any of that."

"Is there anybody else in the building she might've been close to?"

"Honey, I can tell you've never lived in a place like this. Here, you don't *want* to know your neighbors."

"Well, thank you. I'm sorry to have bothered —"

"Aw, it wasn't no bother. I was just watching a dumb rerun of *The Jeffersons.*"

■ ■ ■ ■

TUESDAY,
MARCH 13

■ ■ ■ ■

1:41 a.m.

When I heard the taps on the motel door I went to the window next to it and peered around the dusty curtain. Gregor Deeds, hunched against a strong offshore wind. Quickly I let him in.

"Anything from Hy?" I asked.

"No. He's still out of touch."

I felt a prickle of apprehension. "Who's watching Camilla?"

"Another op — Veronica Mann. I think Camilla's better off with a woman."

"Good choice. I know Ronnie; like you, she's good with anxious people. Any news on Van Hoffman?"

"Some. You got coffee?"

"Pepsi, wine, or beer. All lukewarm."

"I'll take Pepsi."

I poured it for him, and some wine for myself.

Then we perched on opposite sides of the

sagging bed.

"Van Hoffman's still in the hospital," he said. "Our people are keeping a close eye on him, as are the cops and the feds, but his lawyer's shooing them all away."

"Who's the attorney?"

He mentioned a well-known Peninsula ambulance chaser.

Deeds added, "His wife and daughters haven't visited him. In fact, nobody has."

"Doesn't surprise me; he's not a likable man."

"That's not all. An exhaustive check of FBI records — arranged for us by your Mr. Morland — confirms that both Van Hoffman and the Global Policy Forum possessed no information that could jeopardize national security. They are, in fact, losing their funding after the first of the year."

"Your contacts tell you anything about them?"

"They're supposed to be this high-toned think tank studying how our government should run, but nobody listens to them. What they seem to do really well is spend the taxpayers' money on unnecessary travel and expensive vehicles and high salaries."

"Like a lot of our legislators."

"Right. But they seem to have overstepped. Funding has been cut off and they're disbanding in June. They were a creation of the previous presidential administration, and tolerance is low in this one."

I thought of the shabbiness of the Hoffman home on the Peninsula, the low amount of the ransom demand. He must have been deferring maintenance in advance of a salary cutoff. Still . . .

"Are you sure they'll really disband?"

"As far as the public goes, yes."

"What does that mean?"

"They're fanatics, and likely to continue their activities independently."

I said, "I happen to know that there are any number of covert organizations operating under any number of government umbrellas that have activities and information that even the White House isn't aware of."

"You came by this exclusive knowledge from the old Rip?"

"No. Let's just say I worked a case once, and leave it at that."

"Okay. But I still believe that with Hoffman and his Forum, the claims of access to secrets were for show, and their power started to erode years ago. With the help of the Night Searchers they're staging all this weird stuff to shore up their public image."

"I don't understand."

"Well, if there seems to be a distinct threat

to Hoffman and the Forum from a band of renegades who creep around at night and do weird things, their claim to possessing secrets seems more valid. They may even have made up secrets that they'll present to whoever controls their funding in the future."

"Seems a very convoluted way of keeping their jobs."

"Unless they need those jobs to carry out an agenda."

"Oh, God, Gregor, this is getting too damn complicated."

"Not for your mind. The old Rip's told me about the way it works."

I drew my legs up, put my forehead on my knees. "It's not working so well now. I can't fathom what that agenda might be."

"Neither can I."

"Next step," I said. "Lay a trap. Make them play their own game — but one of our own devising."

"That's gonna take some creativity."

"Creativity is my agency's stock in trade."

3:09 a.m.
The folks at McCone Investigations often come together to brainstorm. As many of us who can, convene and let the creative juices flow and blend to provide a possible solu-

tion to a particularly stubborn problem. Now, in the early hours of the morning, we couldn't all be together in a physical sense, but with Mick's and Derek's expertise, we held a virtual meeting, by way of our computers.

I was seated, my back against the wall, on the saggy futon in Mick's old condo. Now that he didn't actually live in the place, he'd turned it into a technophile's dream: monitors covered the walls; keyboards covered every flat surface, even the counters of the tiny galley kitchen; I wasn't surprised to find a screen in the tiny bathroom.

Rae came on first. "I've got the still photos from the Bay-side. They show conclusively that Hoffman jumped into the water and Shar saved him."

"Good work," I told her.

Next Derek. "That 'big, ugly guy' who was trying to find out from the waterfront bum where you'd moved the agency is Gar Diggers. A minor enforcer for any number of scumbags. I'm tracing his movements."

"Thanks."

Julia: "The Kenyons are gone to Amsterdam; I checked with the airline. Chad says he'll be in touch when he gets back."

"Lucky you."

"Lucky? I hope you mean that sarcastically. All Chad's into is stuffing his lasagna hole. I'm starting a diet."

"Good luck with the diet. I'll find you a new assignment tomorrow."

"Nothing to do with food."

Ted: "The guys in suits still come around the office, but not as often now."

"Good. Next time, chase them away."

Patrick: "About Jay Givens's friend out in the Avenues at Balboa and Sixteenth: apartment's leased in Givens's name. Neighbor says a woman lives there. 'Witchy,' she called her. They don't speak, and she doesn't know her name."

"Description?"

"Black hair, pale skin, dark lipstick. Wears jeans and T's and parkas in cold weather. That's it."

"Keep on it."

Derek again: "Van Hoffman's girlfriend. Not much to work on, but I've made a little headway."

"What?"

"I'd rather not say prematurely."

"Okay." I'd learned to trust my operatives' instincts.

"Erica," I asked, "what about Camilla Givens?"

"All she's done is shop."

"Find out what she buys, if any of the

people who help her in the stores know her well. Any ID on the woman she had lunch with on Saturday?"

"Her best friend, Anita Glynn. It's a regular thing most weekends for them to meet there, the waitstaff at Pauline's Precious Tea Room say."

"Pauline's Precious Tea Room?"

Erica shrugged. "Could anybody make that up?"

I looked at my notes. "Okay, Suzy Cushing, Jane Hoffman's niece. Anybody got anything on her?"

"She checks out exactly as she presented herself to you," Mick said.

"Good. I like her."

"What about something for me?" Rae asked.

"I want you on call in case I need you."

She shot back, "Which brings up a question: what're you reserving for yourself?"

"I'm not sure yet. I've got to get deeper into these files. And I need results from all of you first."

I hated to lie to them, but the reasons I was going to be investigating Glenn Solomon were complex and probably — I hoped — invalid.

"Then Team McCone had better get going," Patrick said.

Team McCone. He'd coined a phrase I'd never get rid of.

The screens went black, and I sat there, feeling I'd betrayed them all. And my friend Glenn too.

Mick said, "What's wrong?"

". . . Nothing."

"Liar."

"Really — nothing."

But thoughts of the other day about Glenn echoed in my mind: *contrary to his upright image in the community he was not above a little chicanery in the interests of justice.*

I didn't think that Glenn had been into any criminal activity, but he'd brought me the Givens case with a vague explanation that, after all that had happened since, didn't make a whole lot of sense.

He'd claimed he hadn't known the Givenses well, and that he had assumed they'd come to him because of his friendship with Jay's father in college. He'd said that when they brought him Camilla's "extremely unbelievable tale" he sensed something that he couldn't put into words. Something that was "hinky." At that point I should have sensed something was also hinky about Glenn's story, but when you're dealing with old friends sometimes you ignore your instincts or make allowances for them.

244

But I needed more to go on than suspicions. Glenn respected facts. I'm more likely to give a straight answer if I'm presented with a few myself.

Mick said, "You want to sleep here tonight?" He had his jacket on, was ready to go home to Alison.

Suddenly I felt achingly alone.

Here I was, leading the life I'd chosen. Being free, doing what I loved to do. What did it matter if I spent the night on a lumpy futon or in a fleabag motel with a .357 Magnum as my sole companion? I'd still spend several sleepless hours trying to connect facts that might spell the end of one of my oldest and most cherished friendships.

"I'll stay," I told Mick. "Thank you."

10:33 a.m.

In the morning I commandeered some of Mick's computer equipment and looked into Glenn's story.

I was right to do my research before I spoke with him: there *had* been something hinky about his actions. I called his home; he wasn't there, so I talked to his wife, Bette Silver. Turned out Glenn knew the Givens couple better than he'd claimed. They had been occasional visitors to the Givens's home, and Glenn was Jay's godfather.

Had Glenn recently mentioned them to her? I asked her. The answer was no, not in a month or more, but that wasn't unusual.

"Why aren't you asking Glenn about the Givenses?" Bette said.

"I didn't want to disturb him at the office. Tuesdays, you know . . ."

"Do I ever. The only reason you caught me at home was that a couple of clients canceled on me." Bette was a high-end interior decorator.

"What do you think of the Givenses?"

"Jay makes me nervous; I've always intuited he has hidden agendas. Camilla . . . she's a little intense for my taste."

"Has she gotten more intense recently?"

"You could say so. Glenn told me there was some strange business about a horse on Lombard Street and . . . I don't know what. He says she fantasizes."

"Can you think of anything that's changed in her life that might make her fantasize more than usual?"

"No, but we're not really close." She paused. "There was some legal thing about her that came up last fall. Jay talked it over with Glenn, but it turned out it was a matter Jay could easily handle on his own. Why don't you ask Glenn? I really shouldn't have mentioned it at all."

"Confidentiality."

"Right."

"Sometimes I hate that word."

"So do I."

Okay, I thought after we ended the call, *Glenn lied to me. But he doesn't lie unless he has very good reason to. Does he have some information that he feels will mislead me? Or prejudice me? Or skew my investigation? Or incriminate himself?* And then there was the legal question about Camilla that Jay had consulted Glenn about, that he then decided he could handle himself. What?

The files. The answer might be in the Givens files Glenn had let me read on his computer — the ones I'd printed out when my eyes started to hurt from staring at the glowing screen. The files that I still had in my office . . .

11:45 a.m.

"Rae, I need you to get me some files from my office."

"Sure. Anything else?"

"Lunch?"

"Why did I even ask? Burgers? Fries? Tacos?"

"Tacos!"

"Where're the files?"

"Top drawer in cabinet one. Key's taped

to the bottom of my computer keyboard."

"Where any idiot could find it."

"Files. Tacos. Ginger ale and lots of ice."

"Wait a minute — are you still at Cockroach Haven?"

"Oops! I forgot to tell you — I've moved into Mick's old condo."

"Be there in a flash."

12:31 p.m.
The tacos were great.

While we ate, I paged through the files. It didn't take long to find the first mention of Jay Givens, from some three and a half months earlier. In Glenn's cryptic style it said, "JG was contacted by an HH — David Turnbull — and didn't know what to do. Turnbull is reputable, so I suggested he respond directly and waived my fee."

"HH?" I said. "What's that mean?"

"Don't know. David Turnbull." Rae was tapping on one of Mick's keyboards. "Nothing in the business pages." More tapping. "Or in the residential."

I went to Google. No David Turnbull in the city or Bay Area. Next I tried a general search: many David Turnbulls, so many I didn't know where to start. "Well, hell," I said.

"Yeah, and not as many people are

248

Google-able as you might suppose, so that leaves plenty more. Also, he could've died or left the country or gone to ground or never been that important —"

"That's encouraging." I got up, started pacing around the room. "I'll turn it over to Derek or Mick." I flopped onto the bed. "You know . . ."

"What?"

"There's only one of the Night Searchers we haven't seen in person — Brother Timothy, the Mantis who prays. My sources tell me he's usually around Civic Center Plaza at this time of day."

2:39 p.m.
The Civic Center Plaza is bounded by city hall, the former main branch of the public library (now the Asian Art Museum), and various other important city buildings of the Beaux Arts period. Regrettably, it is also in close proximity to the Tenderloin, San Francisco's skid row, and the spillover has taken the shape of homeless encampments, trolling prostitutes, panhandlers, and crazies.

Crazies such as Brother Timothy "Praying" Mantis.

Just my luck: today Brother Timothy was nowhere in sight.

Rae had dropped me at the plaza in Erica's beater car and promised to come back in an hour. I was wearing my hippie clothing and facial bandages, so there was scant likelihood of anybody recognizing me — including members of my immediate family. I sat on a bench, moved to another, studied the people around me. Plenty of odd individuals — including my own disguised self — but no one in a long robe and bare feet dancing to his inner music.

4:51 p.m.
"Damned unproductive day," I said to Rae. I was resting in a thick terry cloth robe on Mick's lumpy futon, having showered to wash away the scent and feel of Cockroach Haven.

"So what do we do now?" she asked.

"Nothing yet."

Rae was silent, considering possibilities. "Why don't we round up everybody who's free and have another conference — if they're not all off attending to that gargantuan list of tasks you set for them."

6:17 p.m.
Of course, nobody was available. I chafed at the delay, lying on Mick's saggy futon. After a while I watched a movie on the Hulu

channel; it was so mindless and forgettable that it had almost ended when I realized I'd seen it before. I dropped in on a soap opera that had amused me in college, but I didn't recognize any of the characters and couldn't figure out the plot.

And I desperately wished Hy were there.

In the beginning we'd worked so closely that we'd almost died in a mountain mine that had been wired with explosives. Later he'd disappeared and I'd thought he'd been murdered, but I'd found him alive in Mexico and rescued him. We'd nearly frozen to death in the northern Minnesota wilderness. There had been other brushes with danger — close and not so close, together and not together — but we'd survived them all.

So why did I feel this urgent need for him now? Well, I was worried about him — he'd been out of touch for longer than usual. I tried to comfort myself by remembering other dangerous situations I'd emerged from unscathed. Christ, I'd crashed a plane in the rough crags of the Imperial County desert and walked away from it — minutes before it blew up. Held off vicious people armed with baseball bats, guns, and knives. Fended off *coyotes* on the US/Mexican border. All on my own.

251

But maybe I didn't want to be on my own any more.

I could rely on the strongest and most loyal team of operatives I'd ever hoped to assemble. But I still wanted Hy.

Was that feeling dependence? Trust? Weakness? Love?

Or something else that I hadn't yet begun to understand?

When Mick returned from wherever he'd been and set up the conference, he intuited that I wasn't up to leading the session, so he took over. "The Night Searchers canceled tonight's game and are planning to play tomorrow night in honor of Grizeldy. I got that from their website. From the activity on the site I expect more than the usual number of players will turn out."

"Like all of us," Julia said.

"Well, yes. These games aren't easy to pull off; they require a lot of preparation. Clues have to be decided on. Their placement — especially when there're several paths of searching — can be difficult. Derek and I are working out a couple of schemata that seem viable. But we're not ready to go into them yet."

As the others clamored for details, I held up my hands. "Okay, tomorrow's going to be a long day. Let's break this up and go to sleep early."

Of course I didn't take my own advice, but phoned my friend Lonnie Grey from Richman Labs and asked her for more detailed information on the chemicals she'd found in the cigarette lighter I'd asked Richman to analyze.

"Okay, let me check my notes." After a moment she said, "Just what is it you're looking for?"

"Butane is a normal lighter fluid, right?"

"Correct. In itself, butane is relatively harmless, unless inhaled in large amounts. But as I wrote in my report, when it's mixed with certain common household chemicals as reactants and juiced up with a propellant, it can be deadly — or produce some unwelcome results, such as hysteria, paranoia, temporary memory loss, psychosis, or death by asphyxia."

"And what were the reactants in the lighter?"

"Cocaine, phencyclidine — that's commonly called PCP — and disulfiram — used to treat chronic alcoholism. Any of them in a larger-than-prescribed dosage can be problematic for the psyche. The combination of all three would really mess with a

253

person's mind and body."

"And how would these get into a lighter?"

"You mix up a cocktail of them, funnel them in as you would ordinary fluid, and give them a little shake. Simple."

"How many people d'you think are aware of this?"

"God knows. Chemists, if they thought about it. Doctors too. Anybody intelligent who has access to the Internet."

"Pretty scary."

"You bet."

"None of the ingredients is difficult to procure, right?"

"Yep. With or without a prescription."

"And the proportions to achieve the desired effects are also on the Net?"

"Sure." Keyboard noises. "I'm pulling up a site that lists various dosages, from 'Sleepless Nights' to 'Kill.' "

"Jesus," I said, "there has to be some way to regulate this kind of material."

"It's not going to happen until somebody figures out how to regulate the Net."

"And that's not going to be easy." But as I spoke, I thought of Mick and Derek and others of their kind; they'd be the ones who'd do it, if anybody could.

9:52 p.m.

After I talked with Lonnie I actually dozed for a while. Mick's condo might have been shabby, but it was a far cry from an eerily silent and cold motel at the edge of the even colder sea. Still, the cops and FBI had been here earlier, and I had no assurance that they wouldn't bust in at any time with warrants. Already I'd been here too long.

Sure enough I heard footsteps in the hall, jumped up, and stepped behind the door. It swung back and smacked me on the nose.

"Shar?" Mick's voice called out. "Are you here?"

I stepped out, rubbing my nose. "I'm here. But I really can't stand any more facial disfiguration."

He put his hand under my chin and studied my face. "No visible damage."

"It *hurts.*"

"Sorry. But what were you doing back there?"

"I heard you coming and, well, you could've been anybody."

"You can relax. I think some pressure's come down from on high — maybe D.C. — to leave the places you frequent alone. I'd still keep a low profile, but listen to this: I made contact with Brother Timothy. The guy's really whacked out."

"That's no surprise."

"Thing is, he was in love with Grizeldy and thinks the other Searchers 'did something' to cause her death. He's turned on them. Plus I paid him off handsomely."

"With agency money."

"Come on, Shar. You know we can afford it."

"So what'd he tell you?"

Mick's eyes shone: another investigative coup. "He's assigned to plant the clues for tomorrow night's search, and he's offered to take us along. I brought him back on my bike, and he's waiting in the company van."

10:37 p.m.

Brother Timothy smelled: onions, garlic, sweat, tooth decay, and other noxious things. Even though he was seated in the back seat of the van, he polluted Mick's and my environment in the front. The night was cold, but we cracked our windows anyway. Then Mick turned on the blowers and finally the air conditioning. It helped — some.

Timothy had a badly drawn map. He consulted it, then directed me to go southeast on Market Street, passing the dazzling view of lower San Francisco.

"We must take ourselves to the heights,

the Lord sayeth," he announced.

Mick and I exchanged glances.

"Turn, turn, turn — here!" he yelled, and I took a sharp right onto an obscure residential side street, the car behind nearly rear-ending us.

"Can you give me a little more advance notice?" I asked.

"All is in time with God." He paused, then exclaimed, "There it is! That's the house. Pull up."

I pulled to the curb and cut the engine.

"Come on!" He bounded from the back seat, and I followed.

The house was dilapidated and looked in danger of sliding down on its neighbors below. It smelled of dry rot, animal droppings, and skunks.

"It's abandoned," Timothy whispered. "Can you imagine abandoning a place with these million-dollar views?"

"Maybe the owner couldn't pay the mortgage or fix it up."

"Anybody can fix things, unless they are the Children of Darkness." He stopped on the front walk, stuffed one of the familiar envelopes under a cracked paving stone. "Let's go."

The strange mixture of the biblical phrases — which I wasn't at all sure were exact quotes — and contemporary speech made me shake my head as if to clear it. It didn't help.

Next stop: a closed-down convenience store on West Portal, near the Muni tunnel. The rest of the street looked lively, lights sparkling from restaurants, bars, and shops that stayed open late.

"Can you figure how God could let them go bust?" Timothy asked, meaning the convenience store. "Right here by the tunnel, when people're coming home and remember the daily bread they forgot to pick up for dinner?"

The envelope went under a clay pot filled with dead flowers.

Then we were speeding toward the beach. Mick offered to drive, but I told him no. I like the feeling of being in control in a moving vehicle.

Mantis directed me to one of the streets in the Avenues — in the Forties, because I could smell the sea. We stopped in front of a corner home with a turret that made it look like a dwelling out of *Snow White and the Seven Dwarfs.* He dug into his stash of envelopes, handed one to me, and said, "You put it under the doormat."

I took the envelope, went up the steps. The house had the same neglected feel as the last one. I bent down and lifted the doormat, pantomimed putting the envelope under it, but actually stuffed it into my jeans pocket. That'd screw the Night Searchers up, maybe give me time to find out what the mysterious prize was. We continued on to two more sites — one on Cabrillo on the other side of the park, the other on Clay Street, up the hill from Polk Gulch. There Mantis got out of the van and hurried away.

Mick pressed the buttons to open all the windows. "We're gonna have to get this van fumigated," he said.

11:48 p.m.
Team McCone, as they insisted on calling themselves, was assembled on the Internet. I filled them in on Mick's and my evening, then said, "I stole one of the clues Timothy asked me to plant. That'll confuse them."

I took the envelope I'd been supposed to leave under the doormat in the Avenues and read it to them: "Where the wild things are."

"The zoo?" Rae asked.

"Seal Rock?" Patrick.

Adah: "Golden Gate Park?"

"A popular nightclub?" Mick suggested.

Adah laughed. "Maybe it's my mom and dad's place." As of then, her parents possessed three cats, two dogs, two rabbits, and a one-eyed guinea pig. At some point I expected to see an aardvark slink through their living room.

I yawned, fading fast.

"So what're you going to do tomorrow?" Mick asked.

"Confront Glenn Solomon about his omissions. See if he can get the law to lay off of me. I want to go home. I want to see my cats. I'm tired of running."

"We can always . . ."

But the rest of Adah's words were lost to me. I was asleep.

■ ■ ■ ■

WEDNESDAY,
MARCH 14

■ ■ ■ ■

9:10 a.m.

Glenn Solomon was ducking my calls. I could tell from the evasive note in his receptionist's voice. No, his secretary and paralegals weren't available either. No, she didn't know when any of them would be.

Gregor Deeds claimed he had no influence with local law enforcement — which was probably the truth. He was keeping tabs on Camilla Givens, who seemed to be putting down roots in the RI hospitality suite.

"She drinks wine — as much of it as we'll allow — eats popcorn, and watches bad movies," he told me. "According to Veronica Mann, she hasn't said a word about her husband."

"Well, just make sure she stays there."

"I don't think you could get her out with a crowbar."

"Has Hy checked in yet?"

Gregor's voice turned somber. "No, he

hasn't. Still deep into the hostage negotiation."

"Yeah."

Or dead.

No, don't you dare think that way!

9:55 a.m.

Nothing out of the ordinary was going on
at the agency, Ted told me, except for
another invasive visit from guys in suits, and
calls from reporters. Normally that would
be good news, but now I needed to be busy,
to keep my mind off of Hy.

I went down the list of people I should
call and question, finally settled on Suzy
Cushing, who was likely to be the most
forthcoming and friendly of them all. She
was my only entrée into the Hoffman household.

This time she answered her phone. When
I identified myself, she said, "I was just
about to call you. Everything all right?"

"So far."

"Well, I have some news — Uncle Van
checked out of the hospital this morning
and came home. The FBI has him under
surveillance, though."

"How is he?"

"He's gone into one of his silent states,
won't talk to anybody from the law or

264

government and seems particularly angry with Aunt Jane. I heard him talking on the phone to someone named Pamela earlier — mentioning broken promises and betrayed trust. I think he may have been, as they say, disappointed in love."

So it appeared to be over with the girl-friend.

"Suzy, has he ever mentioned an organization called the Night Searchers?"

". . . No, I don't think so."

"Have you heard any of these names?" I read off my list, starting with Jay Givens.

"None is familiar except I remember him talking on the phone to somebody named Jill. It sounded as if he was trying to calm her down."

"When was this?"

"A few weeks ago. Three, maybe?"

"Do you remember anything else about the conversation?"

". . . No. But I'll call you if I find out anything."

10:54 a.m.

Mick phoned me shortly after I finished talking with Suzy. Jay Givens had called the office, saying he "desperately" needed to talk with me in person.

"Well, he can't come here, not to your

place. But it has to be someplace secure, with monitoring devices —"

"What about Cockroach Haven?"

"No. It's a safe house. Nobody goes there except for RI insiders and clients." I hesitated. "Are the feds still sniffing around the offices?"

"Ours, but not RI's."

"Tell him to come there. And pick me up in the van. I'll sneak in the back way."

12:03 p.m.
Jay Givens looked puzzled when RI's receptionist ushered him in to Hy's office, which I'd co-opted.

"What the hell is this place, and what are you doing here?" he asked.

"It belongs to an associate of mine." I motioned for him to come inside.

Jay was dressed in an elegant gray suit with a blue shirt and tie. I knew from the fit and fabric of the suit that it was tailor-made and must have cost thousands — a confident power garment. But he wasn't confident at all. He hesitated, then remained standing, crossing his arms over his chest.

"I haven't had a report from you since we last spoke," he said.

"I believe our contract says I only report when I *have* something to report."

"Well, I have plenty to report to you. Camilla's left me."

I pretended innocence. "As of when?"

"Sunday. I was . . . out and returned to an empty condo. I thought she'd gone off on one of her little shopping sprees" — he sneered — "and it wasn't until later that I realized she'd taken quite a few of her things."

"How much later?"

"When I was getting ready for bed."

"And what time was that?"

"Around midnight."

"You thought she'd shopped until *midnight*?"

"I wasn't thinking. About Camilla, I mean. I was thinking about a client's tax problems and watching a TV movie."

"Both at once?"

"Of course not! Look, I know you don't like me, but I'm really concerned about Camilla. I called her friend Anita Glynn, and she hasn't heard from her. And Camilla's been doing it again."

"Doing what?"

"Fantasizing. She called me three times this morning, starting at six o'clock. Wouldn't tell me where she was. First thing she said was that she wanted a divorce. I think I talked her out of it. But then she told me she'd seen a gorilla scaling the Transamerica Pyramid, started crying and hung up. Next it was a man putting a woman's body into a trunk in the opposite building. Finally she told me that there were vicious-looking birds on the wires outside her windows."

I didn't say anything.

"Ms. McCone," Jay said, "the woman needs help. Real help, not just some therapist who will listen to her hysterical babbling for an hour and charge me an enormous sum."

"You mean she needs to be institutionalized."

"Yes. That's why I need you to locate her quickly. I've already spoken with Dr. Edmond Leeds at Serenity Acres in Napa County, and they're holding a place for her."

"I see." I saw a lot of things, and I didn't like a one of them. "Well, I'll do what I can to find her."

"Just bring my wife back to me. That's all I care about."

After he left I said aloud, "He's full of shit."

Mick's voice answered through one of the speakers, "Amen to that."

I smiled; I'd known he wouldn't be able to resist listening in.

"Keep on eavesdropping." I phoned the RI hospitality suite and spoke with Veronica Mann; Gregor had confiscated Camilla's cell phone when they arrived there, and she didn't have access to any others. The calls from Camilla to Jay simply hadn't happened.

"What about access to drugs?" I asked.

"There isn't so much as an aspirin in the place. And I made sure she didn't sneak any in."

I took the lighter that Richman Labs had examined from my jeans pocket. Ran my fingers over its stippled surface. When I raised its lid, it gave off a faint odor of the noxious mixture that had filled it, and I lowered it quickly. "She smoking?"

"Not much. Once in a while she bums a cigarette off me or Gregor, but we insist on lighting it. No way are we allowing her access to fire."

There was no doubt now that Jay Givens was a damn liar. He should've been more imaginative about Camilla's "hysterical babbling." Those stories had come straight out of Hollywood: *King Kong*, *Rear Window*, and *The Birds*.

3:33 p.m.
After I went back to Cockroach Haven, I

spent the day alternately making inquiries — or asking others to do so — and sleeping wrapped in my comforter. Neither my operatives nor I were coming up with anything on Jordan Turnbull, or Dr. Edmund Leeds at Serenity Acres in Napa County, or on any of the other names that had been dropped into the case.

And as each hour passed I became more and more edgy about Hy.

Camilla Givens, one of her keepers said, had been docile all day. She'd switched from popcorn to pistachio nuts, asked for a cheeseburger, and taken a long nap.

"Keep her sedated — with food, not booze."

One blessing, at least.

9:17 p.m.
I wanted my house, my husband — when he finally resurfaced — and my cats. I wanted to reclaim my life. So I packed up my belongings, said goodbye to Cockroach Haven, and went home.

I was more and more determined to put this bizarre case behind me.

Then, maybe, Hy and I could take a vacation. Not a few days at the ranch or the coast, but a real one. Exotic climes, solitude, good love to make, good books to read, good food and drink. We'd never had a time quite like that . . .

The garage door opener didn't work. I pressed it multiple times, tossed it onto the console in frustration, and cut the ignition. I'd have to open it from inside —

As I crossed to the front door, I heard a noise behind me. Just a whisper, but I turned — and something heavy collided with my forehead. Pain erupted and coursed down from my head to my entire body. My vision blurred, my balance vanished, and I fell backward, landing hard on the concrete; worse pain leaped up my spine, and my vision blanked entirely. But I didn't lose consciousness.

I heard a sound close by, smelled something — what? — that was distinctively male . . .

"You want to leave this alone," a guttural voice said close to my ear. "This ain't got nothing to do with you. Just let the Night Searchers do their work. Leave 'em alone."

And then *I* was alone, half blind and throbbing with pain. Tried to concentrate on the man's voice but couldn't.

I got my breathing under control and spent two or three quiet minutes taking in fresh air. Then I pushed up to a sitting position. Again my vision swam, and I closed my eyes, waiting for the spell to pass. Okay, that was all right, but the pain in my back was awful.

When we'd bought this house we'd reveled in the quiet and the low foot and auto traffic of Avila Street. Now I wished someone would come along and help me . . .

Sometime after 10 p.m.
The first person to come to my aid was Kirk Adderly, my neighbor to the right. I was still disoriented and struggling to get up when I heard him say, "Sharon? That you?"

"Me," I managed to get out.

"Are you okay?"

"Not sure."

"Let me get you up and into the house. What happened? Did you fall or —"

"Not important right now."

Kirk squatted down beside me. "Should I call 911?"

"No. Not necessary."

"Is Hy home?"

"Off someplace. Not sure where."

After a couple more minutes I let Kirk help me up. I clung to him, and soon I was standing. I stifled a cry when the pain in my back intensified.

"Easy," he said. "Wrap your arm around my neck while I get the door open."

I handed him my keys and soon we were inside. "Where do you want to go?" he asked.

"Living room couch."

In moments he had me lying there. "Blankets and a pillow," he said. "Where?"

"Linen closet, top of the stairs."

"Ice bags?"

"Freezer in the garage."

"Be right back."

Pain radiated from my neck and the small of my back; I felt as if I were being penetrated by dozens of thick red-hot needles as Kirk lifted me up to slide the ice bags and pillow beneath me. The ice gave me shivers, but the blanket helped some.

"You want something hot to drink? Coffee?" he asked.

"Nothing, thanks."

"Anybody I can call?"

I thought for a few seconds, then gave him Rae's number.

In spite of the pain I was fading fast. I felt a thump on the couch, and little cat whiskers touching my face. Jessie. I tried to put my hand out to pat her, but before we connected, I was out.

■ ■ ■ ■ ■

THURSDAY,
MARCH 15

■ ■ ■ ■ ■

Sometime in the middle of the night . . .
I opened my eyes and found Gregor Deeds watching me. He was seated in an armchair beside our kiva-style fireplace, where flames glowed steadily.

"How you feeling?" he asked.

"Too soon to tell."

"We had that doc RI uses in tricky situations come over and take a look at you. Nothing broken, no serious internal injuries. You remember him being here?"

"Not too clearly."

"He gave you a shot, left some strong pain meds. Wants you to come in for a checkup and X-rays, though."

"Hy?"

"He's still incommunicado."

Damn!

"Don't worry about him, he'll be all right. Worry about yourself. Did you get a look at who attacked you?"

"No. Bastard hit me from behind." I told Deeds what the man had said to me. "Something about him seemed familiar. I'm getting too close to an answer for somebody's comfort."

"Who? Any idea?"

". . . As I said, there was something familiar . . . no, I don't know."

"Think. Was it his face? Clothing?"

"No. It's dark out there; the nearest streetlight is half a block away."

"So it wasn't visual. His voice?"

"I don't think so."

"Touch?"

". . . Maybe. No, I smelled something . . ."

"You smelled something. What?"

". . . Lime juice? Only more bitter."

"Aftershave or cologne?"

"Maybe."

My eyes were closing, and I couldn't talk any more. Deeds started to say something, but I slipped under again.

9:57 a.m.

"Rise and shine, sweetheart." Rae.

"Fuck that."

"You must be feeling better."

"Oh, yeah. I feel ready to jump up and tap-dance."

"Definitely better. We've got scrambled

278

eggs and toast going. Coffee's brewing."

I made a face. "You eat. All I want is a pain pill."

"Okay, but it'll make you sleepy all day."

"I *want* sleep."

"I know you do, but the doc doesn't advise too many of them. It is, however, a good idea for you to rest and stay out of it."

"Stay out of what?"

"We're closing in on the Night Searchers. Gregor and Mick dug up some info."

"Maybe I will have a cup of coffee."

Soon Rae entered with two steaming mugs, and I took the one she held out. "What about the Night Searchers?"

"Mick located Marlene Daniels. She hasn't gone far, just to Oakland. He visited her, had to pay her off to get her to talk. She confirmed that in the last two years the group has been hired by various people to do some nasty stuff. That's the reason she left them."

"Nasty stuff. Such as?"

"Frighten an old couple out of their rent-controlled apartment. Intimidate the victim in a rape case so she wouldn't testify. Entrap a politician — she wouldn't say who — in a compromising situation. Scare a couple of small business owners into giving up their leases. Extract information from somebody in the D.A.'s office about evidence in an upcoming case. And if that's just the tip of the iceberg, we're looking at a lot of misdemeanors and felonies."

"Quite a little cottage industry they've got going there. Did this Zero say who had hired them for these jobs?"

"That she wouldn't tell. Fear of reprisal."

"Well, after last night I understand that all too well. Any idea of who tried to put the fear of the Night Searchers into me?"

"No. I doubt it was one of their more prominent members. Their MO seems to be attracting people in search of adventure and assigning them to unpleasant or illegal tasks. None of them stay with the group long because they're afraid of getting caught."

"I want to talk to Zero."

"Shar, you can barely walk. And if you take one of those pills —"

"So bring her here."

"I don't know if she'll —"

"Ask Gregor if he'll go get her. He looks sufficiently mean."

9:30 p.m.

Marlene Daniels also looked sufficiently mean when Gregor finally led her into my living room. She was short and heavyset, with long wispy gray hair and a caved-in face, and the sides of her eyes and lips didn't match. The back of her head was oddly flattened. The deformities were why she'd never been adopted: shortsighted wannabe parents want perfect babies. Her eyes, muddy brown, glittered as she approached the couch where I was propped up.

"A lot of nerve you've got," she said in a deep-South drawl, "sending this ape to manhandle me." As she spoke, she revealed crooked, yellowed teeth.

This ape.

Not only was she physically deformed, she was also a racist.

I bit back a tart reply along those lines, said to her, "I'm sorry. Please sit down. Somebody assaulted me last night, or else I would've come to you. One of the Night Searchers, I think."

"Well, that's no big surprise." She looked closely at me before she took the chair by the fireplace. "Your guy didn't exactly manhandle me," she relented, "but he scared the hell out of me. Not that that's anything new. I been scared for a while now."

"Since you left the Night Searchers."

"Ran from them, is more like it. They're into some pretty bad shit."

Zero's gaze shifted nervously around the room, stopping at the bookcases, the big-screen TV, the tables and lamps.

"Must be nice," she said, "living in a place like this."

"It's nice, but we haven't been here long. Our old house was set on fire and burned to the ground last year. This one is all new, and so far I don't feel much connection to it."

"You lost everything?"

"Except for our cats and a pair of my grandmother's earrings." I didn't mention my old .38 Special, which along with the earrings had been in my father's navy-issue strongbox bolted to the floor in my linen closet.

"How'd you get all this stuff?"

"Insurance. But that doesn't make up for the family pictures and souvenirs and . . . well, most anything."

"I got no pictures, no family either. Didn't have a home — just a lot of places where people took me in for public money. I guess you could say I got stuff now. Not good stuff, but it's mine. I'd hate to see it burn up like yours did."

Gregor, I saw, was standing in the doorway behind where Zero was sitting. I knew that he was recording my conversation with the woman. He'd told me he would, as RI protocol dictated.

I said to Zero, "Tell me about your time with the Night Searchers."

"You sure I won't get in trouble with the cops for what I done in the past? Your guy told me I wouldn't, but I wanna hear it from you too."

"Whatever you say to me will remain strictly between us."

"All right, then . . . you hear that they're kind of a national organization?"

"Yes."

"Well, I was living in Arkansas — Fayetteville. You know it?"

"As a matter of fact, I do." A case had once taken me there.

"It's a pretty dull town, even with the college. I was sent there to my last foster home before I came of age. The people were awful. They thought I was there to wait on them; a lot of foster families do. I took to hanging out in a park and smoking dope at night after the folks went to bed. And I met what I thought was the coolest bunch of people."

"Night Searchers."

"Yeah. But there they called themselves the Night Fates. Fayetteville, fates — you get it?"

"Uh-huh."

"Well," she went on, "one night the foster dad beat me up because I wouldn't let him . . . you know. And I split with all the money I had saved from this part-time job they didn't even know about. Somebody in the Night Fates had told me about this awesome group out here and gave me Grizeldy's name and address. I caught a Greyhound, rode forever it seems, and the Griz took me in."

"And then?"

"At first it was all fun and games. Then Griz told me I had to start earning my keep. Pulling little scams, that kind of thing. I'd done it before, didn't mind it. If they can be scammed, people deserve what they get. It went along okay, and I got kind of important in the organization. I mean, they'd turn to me for solutions to problems and all. I'm not educated, much, but I'm logical."

"These scams — what were they?"

"Well, this one old lady that a member was doing home care for, she had a lot of valuable stuff. The caregiver would replace it with junky things, we'd sell the real stuff, and the old lady didn't even realize the difference. Phone scams — there were a lot of those. You get somebody's number and some info on them, then you call up pretending to be a relative who's in trouble and needs money. Going door-to-door and asking for donations in cash for a charity that doesn't exist."

"And the victims of these scams — were they mostly elderly people?"

"Of course. They're easy to fool."

Easy to fool. Yes, an unfortunately high percentage of seniors are, but with outreach and educational programs, that's changing. Personally, I think that people who prey on the elderly ought to be incarcerated until they are the ages of their victims.

"Then it got to be not so good," Zero added.

"What went wrong?"

"They started doing these weird night-time excursions, for no reason I could figure out. They didn't ask me along, and I didn't want to go anyway. But I could tell when one was about to go down, because there'd be all this excitement — lots of phone calls, people talking about costumes and note cards. They'd get real quiet around me; I guess what they were doing was really important, and they didn't trust me 'cause I was new to the organization. So I said, 'Fuck this' and found a job and split."

"How long ago was this?"

"Maybe two months. How'd you people

find me?"

"You were described to me by Grizeldy as the leader of the Night Searchers. Why, do you suppose?"

"To protect the real leaders."

"Who are . . . ?"

"Well, the Griz. But Supercom, he's always been top dog."

"What's Supercom's real name?"

"I don't know."

"Jordan Turnbull?"

"Never met anybody called that."

"Who does know?"

She shrugged. "The Griz, I guess."

Zero didn't seem to know that Grizeldy was dead, and I didn't bother to enlighten her.

"Nobody else?"

"Don't think so. The others, well, you've seen them. They seem really flaky, even to somebody like me."

My back was throbbing steadily now, although less painfully. I thanked Zero for her information, then said, "Mr. Deeds will take you back home now. Let us know if you remember something else."

She nodded and stood. "I'm sorry you're hurting. He never should've done this to you."

It took a bit for the way she'd made that

last remark — as if she knew who my at-
tacker was — to register with me. By the
time it did, Zero and Gregor were out of
the house and into his car. Damn, why was
my mind so sluggish?

Didn't matter. Zero wasn't going anyplace. To ensure that, I'd ordered a twenty-
four-hour guard on her house.

11:03 p.m.

"Shar, wake up. Hy's on the phone." Rae,
who had taken over for Gregor and helped
me into bed, thrust the receiver at me.

The rush of relief I felt cleared my head
almost instantly. I'd been asleep for I didn't
know how long — having taken half a pain
pill. I grabbed the phone and uttered a
somewhat fuzzy, "My God, Ripinsky, I
thought I'd never hear your voice again."

"Deeds told me you've had a rough time.
How do you feel?"

"Not bad, now. How and where are you?"

"I'm fine. At JFK, waiting for a direct
flight to SFO."

I let my breath out explosively. "Thank
God!"

He laughed. "This marriage goes on much
longer, and you'll revert to Catholicism."

"Well, I might start believing in hope and

peace and brotherly and sisterly love and —"

"Are you stoned?"

". . . Sort of. Pain pills."

"Then lie there and enjoy it. I'll see you in about seven hours. Love you."

He broke the connection.

"Love you," I said, and switched the phone off. Then I lay there and enjoyed my painless, dreamy state. And it was sometime during it that I had a sudden memory jog.

■ ■ ■ ■

Friday, March 16

■ ■ ■ ■

8:40 a.m.

"Yesterday was the ides of March. Once again, we're safe."

I pushed up instantly, wincing at the pain in my lower back, and stared at Hy's smiling face.

"You know how to scare a woman, Ripinsky!"

"You're not scared." He kicked off his shoes and flopped down next to me.

"All's well?" I asked.

"All's well. A bunch of rebel assholes kidnapped the CEO of an American corporation with offices in São Paulo, Brazil. He's now at home, and they're in the slammer, or whatever they call it down there. Tricky business — that's why I was out of touch so long."

"And you're home too." I threw an arm across his chest and snuggled in by him.

"Home, and dead tired. How's the back?"

"Still achy, but on the mend. Rae's been keeping me immobile with an arsenal of chemical wonders."

"Rae. Oh, yeah, I just kicked her out of the house."

"You *what*?"

"I'm in charge now. She needs her sleep too."

"Ripinsky, this case —"

"Sssh."

"Even with all the pills — or maybe because of them — I've made a connection —"

"Sssh."

His breathing slowed and lapsed into the rhythm that I knew meant deep sleep. Well, why not? I closed my eyes and slept too.

3:30 p.m.

Cheese-and-mushroom omelets. Heaps of bacon. Crispy hash browns.

Thank God I'd married a man who could cook!

Of course, Hy had had to learn; his first wife, Julie Spaulding, had been an invalid — MS — and confined to a wheelchair for the better part of their marriage. Not that she'd let it stop her: she was an environmental activist who had headed organizations such as the Friends of Tufa Lake, and led marches and protests for other ecological causes. As she'd once told Hy, "People are not inclined to attack a gimp in a wheelchair for being a 'tree-hugger.' " A strong, dedicated woman, Julie. I would have liked her.

I dug into the late brunch like a bear after hibernation. Hy did the same. As we ate, I filled him in on everything that had gone down during his absence. "And you know what?" I finished. "Last night, in my drugged state, I remembered something."

"What?"

"That's the trouble. I don't remember now."

"Drug-induced hallucination. You sure you haven't been chomping on some magic mushrooms?"

"Ripinsky, I haven't done that since — well, since too long ago to mention."

He was looking thoughtful. "Sometimes details get lodged in our subconscious until it coughs them up."

"Now you're equating my memory with a hair ball." The latter statement was punctuated by Jessie, walking by on her way to the food bowl.

But he was serious. "You don't have any recollection of this . . . revelation?"

I closed my eyes, thought hard. "No."

"Let's see if we can't get it out of wherever

it's stuck."

I was lying on the couch again, responding to Hy's soft questioning, when a name came to me.

"Jordan Turnbull."

"Who's that?"

"A name from Glenn's files on the Givenses. Glenn called him 'an HH.' That mean anything to you?"

"HH? No, not offhand."

"Glenn said Jay had told him about Turnbull contacting him and suggested Jay deal with it personally. There was no number for Turnbull in the phone directories for the Bay Area; he's not Google-able either."

"And?"

"And that's it. I was going to ask Glenn about Turnbull, but I think he's ducking my calls. Mick said Derek would look into it. He couldn't have gotten far, or I'd've heard by now."

"Could Turnbull be this Supercom that Zero mentioned?"

"Maybe."

"Better put Mick on that too."

"His plate for tonight is full up. He's going out on another mysterious excursion with the Searchers."

Hy frowned. "Are you sure they aren't suspicious of him?"

"He says not. I tried to talk him out of going, but he wouldn't listen. Stubborn, like everybody else in my family."

"Including you. How confident are you of his judgment in the field?"

". . . Pretty confident."

"Well, he better be careful."

"He's stopping by beforehand. I'll warn him. And ask him to remind Derek to keep checking on Jordan Turnbull. And I'll also badger Glenn about him."

"Good. When?"

"Right now."

Hy handed me my cell.

And, once again, Glenn wasn't available.

"He's ducking you all right," Hy said.

"Then I'll just go hunt him down and wrench the truth out of him —" I started to get off the couch, in spite of a protesting twinge in my back.

Hy held me down. "You're not going anywhere yet."

"Oh, yes I am." I struggled out of his grasp. "Don't try to stop me."

He sighed. "All right. But at least wait for Mick's input and give him his instructions. Meantime, you and I can keep kicking around what we know."

Mick had interesting news: he'd canvassed the building in the Avenues where Jay Givens leased an apartment and found out from one of the tenants that the "witchy woman" who lived there was named Opal Carson. She was a chemist working for Personal Solutions, a lab that developed cosmetics, in the East Bay city of Emeryville.

"I've turned Derek loose on her," he said, "and he's to call you with any results."

"Good work. What about this Turnbull character? Did Derek find anything on him?"

"I guess not."

"Check this out too." I held out the note I'd pocketed while planting clues with Brother Timothy.

He read it. "*Where the Wild Things Are.* It's a children's book by Maurice Sendak. I remember it from when I was a kid. It was made into a movie a few years ago."

"What location could this be referring to? And I don't mean the park or the zoo or anywhere else so obvious."

"Hell, it could be my house right now. Alison's adopted two stray cats, and we're not even unpacked yet."

"Think."

"Wild things. This is a city. The Tenderloin?"

"Uh-uh. Those people there aren't wild, so much as drugged out and half dead."

"Lands End?"

"Possibly. But a lot of pedestrians and cyclists go there, even at night."

Mick considered. "You know, there was a lot of attention focused on Mount Sutro Forest when UCSF wanted to thin out the eucalypti and old-growth pines old Adolph Sutro planted there. And now there's some dispute about more development."

The forest, one of the last dreams of the city's most flamboyant millionaires and Mayor Adolph Sutro, covers nearly eighty acres and is mainly composed of huge blue gum eucalyptus, many of them dying. These nonnative trees, imported from Australia, are shallow-rooted and brittle, falling frequently and suddenly in high winds, and therefore dangerous. UC, which owns three-quarters of the forest, had proposed to drastically thin them, as well as remove many of the other nonnative plants that grow on the high hill. The only creatures you were likely to find on Mount Sutro were great horned owls, raccoons, skunks, possums, and feral cats.

"It's pretty wild up there," Hy said.

I sat up. "Let's check it out."

"Are you crazy? It's a dark night. And you're not fit to —"

"We're going to check it out." I lifted myself off the couch without even a twinge this time. "Darkness doesn't matter — I have a night scope and an infrared camera. And you." I looked him in the eye. "You'll help me."

The doubt on his face vanished, was replaced with determination. "Yeah, I'll help you. Haven't we always helped each other?"

9:10 p.m.
"This is a ridiculous idea, you know," Hy said.

"I've done ridiculous before, and it's turned out all right." I ignored the strain on my back as I forged on up the forest trail.

The ground was steep and rocky, edged with low vegetation and blackberry vines that scratched at my ankles. As the trail steepened, I had to stop now and then to rest. To one side the lights of the city and East Bay glistened; to the other, fog billowed in from the Gate and would soon envelop us. Some people liken the odor of eucalypti to cat piss, but to me it's exotic, reminding me of worlds I've never seen. To

298

say nothing of its clearing my clogged si-
nuses.

"Why in hell did Adolph Sutro even *want*
this place?" Hy grumbled.

"Because he wanted every place in the
city. Did you know that at one time he
owned ten percent of the land here?"

"He must've been nuts."

"Of course he was — look at Cliff House,
or Sutro Baths, or Sutro Heights. Cliff
House burned down twice; the seven bath-
ing pools succumbed to high operating and
maintenance costs and are now lying in
ruins; all that's left on Sutro Heights is a
decrepit parapet overlooking the sea."

"McCone, I didn't know you were such a
student of local history."

"All history is fascinating. As you've told
me, we don't know where we are now until
we know what's come before."

We kept forging ahead.

Hy asked, "Do you have any idea where
this clue is hidden?"

"Not exactly. But a pattern to their placement has occurred to me."

"What?"

"The clues are never too far from where
you park your car, and usually in a protected
place."

"So? Aren't there other entrances than the

one we took?"

"Yes. But the ones to the part of the forest UCSF owns aren't open to the public. We came in through the city-owned access point."

"Illegally, after hours."

"True."

We were both silent for a time. Then a frisson moved along my spine that had nothing to do with my earlier injury, and I shivered.

I said, "I swear I just felt Ishi's spirit."

Ishi was the last of the Yahi Indians — a Stone Age tribe. One day in 1911, he walked out of the hills near Mount Lassen and joined the twentieth century. The UC system took him in, and he lived the remaining five years of his life on Parnassus Heights, where he cooperated with UCSF doctors and researchers. It is said he frequently visited Sutro Forest, perhaps because it reminded him of the millennia-old home he'd left behind.

Hy said, "I always thought the old man was scamming everybody."

"Maybe so. I like to think otherwise."

"McCone, you're turning into a romantic."

I stopped abruptly, and he banged into me. "Over there," I said.

"Where?"

"To the right, between those two big trees."

"I see it. A park shelter . . ."

"Perfect spot for a clue."

I'd guessed right: the clue was there — an envelope like the others tucked barely out of sight on the covered bench that overlooked the city lights. Hy held the flashlight while I opened it.

The city lights shine here.

"Great," I said. "City lights're all over the place."

Hy was silent.

"What?" I asked.

"Twin Peaks? Looking down on all the lights?"

"Too obvious."

"Other prominent viewing places?"

"Nob Hill? Coit Tower? Bernal Heights? There're hundreds of those. Wait a minute — City Lights Bookstore?"

He thought that over. "You may have something there."

10:32 p.m.

City Lights Bookstore, on Columbus Avenue in North Beach — and ironically only a stone's throw from where I'd had the incident with Grizeldy's car — is a local landmark and a national literary icon. It began as the country's first all-paperback store and evolved into a venue for poets and writers of the Beat Generation. It is jam-packed with some of the best American, English, and small-press books in print. And it is open until midnight.

Tonight its windows were blurred by incoming fog, but presented a colorful arrangement of newly minted offerings. Hy and I bypassed them and paused inside the store.

"Where're we supposed to look?" he asked.

"Good question."

But one that was easily answered. I went over to the checkout desk, asked if there was a message for an "n.s." — the others had been marked this way. The clerk riffled through a stack of papers and handed me an envelope like the others we'd found.

Outside, in the light from the windows, I opened it. It contained a piece of paper with an address on it: Twenty-Third Avenue in the Sunset district. I recognized it as the home Grizeldy had inherited.

I said, "Why would they send a team to a member's own place?"

"She was the one who designed the hunt and provided the prize?"

"That doesn't sound right." I thought back, remembered Grizeldy saying, as she urged me to go on without her when she had the asthma attack, *That prize is important to me.*

"She knew what the prize was," I said, "but not where it was hidden."

11:19 p.m.

Grizeldy's block, between Moraga and Noriega Streets, was fogbound and dark. The house was your standard stucco two-story, with the main living space on the top floor, an entry and garage on the first. Its windows were covered with blinds, and there wasn't even a security spot or solar light to show the way.

Hy said after we got out of the car, "Okay, now that we're about to become involved in breaking and entering —"

"What do you mean? I have keys." I jingled them lightly.

"How'd you manage — ?"

"I took them from her car when she had her attack the night before she died. I hung on to them, figuring I'd give them to her lawyer or whoever ended up handling her estate."

We moved slowly toward the house and around it, checking for junction boxes that would indicate a burglar alarm. None. Finally we went up the front stairs, and I tried to insert one of the keys. It wouldn't go in. Neither would the second. The third did, and the knob turned. We slipped inside, and Hy closed and locked the door behind us.

"Flashlights?" he asked.

"Till we familiarize ourselves and cover the windows. Then it won't matter: I don't suppose she was friendly enough with her neighbors for them to take note of her comings and goings. And an obituary won't have appeared yet."

The house had probably been built by Henry Doelger, a San Francisco architect whose cookie-cutter, post–World War II homes had proliferated on what used to be sand dunes in the southern reaches of the city. It had the standard layout: bedroom in front, living room, bath, spare bedroom, kitchen, and large all-purpose room — probably an add-on — behind. The front bedroom and living room were empty. The second bedroom and bath and kitchen were furnished sparingly, the back room not at all. Grizeldy had apparently lived only in the kitchen, smaller bedroom, and bathroom.

The blinds that were closed on all the

windows were thick metal, the kind that show little light to anyone outside. "Okay with the electricity," I said to Hy.

He located switches, and suddenly we were seeing the interior in all its neglect.

The kitchen floor was dirty and sticky on the soles of my shoes; the bathroom was worse; the bedding on the single mattress on the floor looked as if it hadn't been washed in at least a year, and clothing was piled in heaps. I wondered if all this filth might have contributed to Grizeldy's bad health. The only clutter-free space was a section of the kitchen counter, where a phone, a fax/printer, and a Dell computer were set up.

I'm good with simple computer tasks, but Hy's better. I asked, "You want to take a look at this?"

He sat down on the stool in front of it.

I went on searching through the poverty of Jill Kennedy's life.

Three large, empty rooms that appeared as if they'd never been used. A closet with no hangers upon which the heaps of clothing could be hung. Randomly squeezed toothpaste tube on the back of the sink, toothbrush that should have been replaced long ago in the holder. Medicine cabinet: should have been revealing, as most are, but wasn't. No prescription drugs, no over-the-counters except Tylenol, no makeup or hairspray or anything else that she might have bought in an attempt to make herself more attractive.

I went back to the kitchen. Hy was still tinkering with the computer, and I didn't interrupt him. The cabinets were reasonably bare: Grizeldy had eaten off a few ancient plastic plates, with cheap, mismatched flatware; there were cans of pork and beans, chili, soup, and spaghetti, but their lids were dusty. The fridge contained a quart of milk two weeks past its sell-by date, a half-full bottle of a particularly vile brand of white wine, and a slice of moldy lemon.

The freezer was more bountiful, if you called three Hungry Man frozen dinners a bounty, along with two partially eaten cartons of ice cream — mint and dark chocolate — and part of a Sara Lee cheesecake. But then . . .

I moved the other items away and pulled at the plastic-wrapped package at the very bottom. It stuck. I tugged at it again, and it came free. There were newspaper wrappings under the thick plastic.

Hy was still busy with the computer. He hadn't made a sound.

I started to open the package, peeling the

wrappings carefully. When finally I freed the contents, I brushed the debris aside to reveal a wooden plaque with a raised plastic center and gold lettering. There are so many plaques given out in this world — I have several — that I wonder if every household doesn't contain a few. But this one was different.

From its front, Grizeldy's — Jill Kennedy's — face stared out at me. She looked solemn and somewhat haunted.

It had been presented to her by the Other Worlds Society on the tenth anniversary of her witnessing her father's alien abduction.

There was a note attached: "Grizeldy, if you find this first, you can have it back for keeps, for services rendered."

How could this plaque be Grizeldy's "grand prize"? It was too damned insignificant . . . and yet witnessing the so-called abduction had been the one event in her life that made her someone of importance. Again, I thought of what she'd told me in the car the night before she died: *. . . a plain, little, ordinary woman. Living a plain, little, ordinary life.*

The sadness and emotional poverty that I often encounter in my work overwhelmed me, and I had to blink to keep tears from my eyes.

■ ■ ■ ■

SATURDAY, MARCH 17

■ ■ ■ ■

Midnight

Somewhere close by, a church bell was tolling the beginning of a new day.

I stood at the shabby kitchen counter, staring down at Grizeldy's plaque.

I said, "Ripinsky, come look at this."

He slipped off the stool and peered at the plaque. "The Other World Society," he said.

I took out my iPhone and checked out the name on Google. "There're two," I said, "but one's called the Other World Society and is devoted to the supernatural. The Other Worlds Society, plural, is concerned with alien abductions."

"Which Grizeldy — Jill, whatever — claimed had happened to her father."

"Right. Anything useful on her computer?"

"Just e-mails notifying people of their ventures. I'm going to print out their names and addresses."

I searched Google for additional mentions of the Other Worlds Society. There were several, most of them dismissive. A few were enthusiastic, but the writers sounded unbalanced. The organization's official site ran profiles of people whom the group claimed might have been spirited away into outer space. Few names, except for Judge Crater and Jimmy Hoffa, rang a bell. Still, I bookmarked the site; I'd read the profiles later at my leisure.

Hy came up behind me. "I'm done here."

"Me too."

"Home?"

"Yes, please."

We left the house and I relocked the door. As we walked toward the car, my cell rang. Jay Givens, sounding frantic. "It's Camilla. She came home and trashed the condo!"

"You weren't there?"

"No. I was out. When I came back the place was trashed and Camilla has the only other key."

"I'll get right back to you."

I clicked off, then called the RI hospitality suite. The voice that answered after six rings was sleep-blurred and unfamiliar. "Camilla Givens — is she there?" I asked.

"Who's this?"

"Sharon McCone, one of the owners of

RI. Who are you?"

"Seth Over. I'm new —"

"Who authorized you to take this shift?"

"Veronica Mann. She had a date —"

"Never mind. Check on our client."

The receiver dropped with a clunk. *Heads are going to roll,* I thought.

Pretty soon Over said, "Ms. McCone?"

"*Is* she there?"

"Um . . . no."

"Search the entire suite, including the closets."

Minutes passed. I filled Hy in on what was happening.

"Ms. McCone? She's definitely not here."

"And you, Mr. Over, are fired."

"What? You can't do that —"

"As co-owner of the firm, you bet I can. You have fifteen minutes to clear out, and you'll receive your last paycheck by mail."

Hy was grinning at me as I disconnected. "You're tougher than I am."

"The guy's a fool — probably sleeping or watching a video when she contrived to slip out. And Veronica Mann — she goes too."

"Whatever you say, boss."

"My God, Camilla's on the loose. No telling what harm she might do to herself or others."

"You going to call her husband back?"

"I'm bound to; he's my client."

"You didn't tell him where she was before."

"Because I thought she was safe. And because I think she has reason to be afraid of him."

"So now she trashed their condo. Why?"

"I have only Jay's word about that, and he's lied to me before. Want to bet the place is in perfect condition?"

"He'd say he got a cleaning crew in."

"This late? I don't think so."

"Did he tell you exactly when the trashing supposedly happened?"

". . . No. I'll call and tell him I'm following up on a lead. And then I'll go over there."

"No, *we'll* go over there."

"Ripinsky, you really are determined to form a partnership with me, aren't you?"

He just smiled.

1:33 a.m.

The Givenses' condo *had* been trashed. Broken glass and overturned furniture and torn-down draperies lay everywhere. In the master bedroom the mattress had been flipped, the drawers emptied out; in a second bedroom that was used as an office, the computer and its ancillary devices had been battered. The worst destruction was in the kitchen: small appliances looked as if they'd been stomped on; frozen food lay melting amid the rubble; pottery shards and more broken glass and dented pots and pans intermingled on the floor.

As Hy and I walked through all this, I knew we were thinking the same thoughts:

Why destroy your own things, such as crystal and china, that probably mean nothing to Jay?

Why ruin your own computer, since Jay told us he mainly uses his laptop or the one in his office?

Why rip up your own clothing, while leaving his relatively intact?

Why, in your private bathroom, smash your mirror with your own bottle of costly perfume?

Rage, of course. But not Camilla's.

We questioned Jay. He had no idea where his wife was now, he said. He hadn't called the police because he was afraid of bad publicity, people prying into his life, and upheaval in his home, and he felt a migraine coming on. We told him we would try to locate Camilla and left.

"His doing," I said.

"His, or somebody who has it in for him or Camilla. Where d'you suppose she is?"

"Maybe back at the suite."

"I'll check." He took out his phone, auto-dialed. Asked a security guard to check to see if she was there. Waited a few minutes, then handed the phone to me.

"Ms. McCone?" the RI man said. "Mrs. Givens returned half an hour ago."

"She say where she'd been?"

"Only that she was getting her life straight."

"Let me talk to her, please."

"I'll get her."

Long silence.

"Ms. McCone, she refuses to come to the phone. Wants to talk with you in person — tomorrow."

"Tell her I want to talk with her *now.*"

"She's in the Jacuzzi tub, and the door is locked."

I felt an overwhelming desire to drive over there, kick the door in, and drag Camilla out of the tub by her whisk-broom hair.

"Well," I finally said, "make sure she stays put."

"She's very willful."

"Then get hold of the RI doctor. After her absence, she needs a physical checkup. And a shot that will put her out for a good eight hours of sleep."

316

3:01 a.m.

Hy and I talked over the situation at home, discussing what my next plan of action should be. I wanted to establish a definite connection between Jay Givens and Van Hoffman and, barring that, a connection between both men and the Night Searchers. We discussed the best way to accomplish that, but couldn't come up with a viable solution.

Mick called around three thirty. "I'm in the men's room at one of those horrible all-night restaurants, so this has got to be quick. The Searchers are ending up at Grizeldy's house tonight; the last clue indicated the big prize is there."

"How'd you find out that?"

"Kilkarzo let it slip while we were at the urinals. He's the one who wrote the clues."

"So why doesn't he just go there and grab this prize?"

"I think because, more than the others, he's the one who really believes in this game. He's simpleminded and really cared about the Griz."

"But he told you their final destination tonight."

"He's also pretty drunk."

"Are you sure they aren't setting it up to lose you? Send you to the wrong place?"

"You're always talking about your gut instincts. Well, I've got them too."

"Yeah, you've proven that. Can you duck out on the Searchers?"

"Sure. I doubt that they want me around anyway."

"Do it, and wait outside Grizeldy's house in the agency van. Hy and I will be inside, and there'll be others outside. Call me when you see the Searchers approaching."

I began marshaling everyone on my phone. Those I was able to reach would be staking out Grizeldy's house when Hy and I arrived to wait for the Night Searchers.

3:40 a.m.

Hy and I were again inside Grizeldy's lonely, barren house. We sat in the dark, empty room at the rear, our backs against the wall.

By now Team McCone was in place: Mick in the agency van across the street; Julia on the walkway to the house's left; Craig and Adah at different locations in the backyard. Patrick hadn't been able to get somebody to look after his two boys, until Rae volunteered; I knew she was chafing at being left out of the action. Even our newbie, Erica, was stationed nearby, alternately nervous and excited.

The Searchers still weren't there. What were they waiting for? Of course, Mick had said they were at a restaurant, and I hadn't thought to ask him where. Maybe they were taking a long time with their meal, or the place was on the other side of the city. Still, the wait was making me edgy.

We'd been there fifteen minutes when my phone vibrated. Derek. I answered in a low voice.

"Opal Carson didn't show up for work today," he said. "I'm keeping watch on her building, but she's not there either."

"You find out anything more about her?"

"Nothing important. The woman doesn't seem to have much of a life outside her work as a chemist."

"Well, keep me posted."

After I broke the connection, I lapsed into silence. Hy put his arm around me, drew my head down onto his chest.

Minutes later, he said, "They're not coming."

"If they are, it's taking a damn long time."

"Maybe the other team'll come. We never did spot any of their clues."

"I'm not sure there *is* another team. Have any of us heard their names, seen them?"

"No." He shifted his arm around my shoulders. "But what purpose would they have in creating a fictional team?"

"Phantoms to put the blame on in case they got caught? An alleged team that vanishes when others come looking for them?"

"You may have something there. Maybe they also created Supercom."

"Very possibly." My cell vibrated. Mick.

"There're three people in dark clothing coming along the block. Being very quiet and looking kind of furtive."

"Keep the line open."

Long pause. Then: "They just passed under a streetlight and I caught sight of them. Kilkarzo, Alinzsky, Malanzky. They've started across to the house."

"Inform everybody outside." I broke the connection, said to Hy, "They're on their way."

We stood up and retreated to a recess beside the long-unused fireplace. Hy unholstered his .45. Regretfully I took out my own weapon. Another promise to myself broken.

Soft footsteps coming up to the front door. A key turning in the lock. The door being shut and locked behind them. I turned on my ultra-sensitive voice recorder.

First person: "So where do we start?"

Second: "Easy. I been here before. She

only lived in three rooms — little bedroom, bathroom, and kitchen."

"Bathroom? Toilet tank? That's where I keep my dope."

"I don't think this is dope, but you take the bathroom, Kilkarzo."

A third voice said, "I'll take the bedroom. Broads always hide stuff in their bedrooms."

"Thanks for your wisdom, Alinzsky. I'll do the kitchen."

The speaker, presumably Malanzky, moved into the kitchen. "Jesus," he said, "gross." Then he began to rip it apart, breaking dishes and glassware, emptying out drawers. Finally he said, "Oh yeah! Of course," and pulled open the freezer. There was the sound of rock-hard foods being tossed onto the filthy floor.

"Oh, man," Malanzky said in a soft voice that wouldn't carry to his partners, "what's this?"

Ripping and tearing noises. A silence. And then an exclamation of rage.

"A plaque? A fucking plaque? *This* is what she was so eager to get her claws onto?"

The others heard him, rushed in.

Malanzky's voice rose even higher. "The bitch had us running all over the city for this valuable thing that was gonna make us all rich. And look at it — a fucking plaque about her father's so-called alien abduction."

Kilkarzo's voice was more tempered. "That so-called alien abduction was the defining moment in the Griz's life. But what does this note mean? 'If you find this first, you can have it back for keeps, for services rendered?' Who was the Hider when we went looking for this? And why did he hide it in her own house?"

"Who the fuck cares?"

Kilkarzo asked, "*What* services rendered?"

Malanzky answered, "We done a lot of services for a lot of people and been paid real good too."

"But this is different. This is something special we did. Like we're supposed to do tomorrow night."

Alinzsky said, "I'm not putting on any more acts in that vacant lot! I'm splitting tonight for my sister's place in Yuba City."

Hy and I stepped out from the recess, weapons leveled.

They froze, then exchanged panicky looks. Alinzsky muttered, "Oh, shit."

Hy and I moved toward them.

"Those acts in the vacant lot — what were they?" I asked.

Silence.

I questioned them about the services

they'd provided for other people. More looks passed between them and they remained mute. I asked about what they were supposed to do in the vacant lot tomorrow. Defensively they folded their arms across their chests.

Alinzsky said, "You're not the cops. We don't have to talk with you."

I told them that was true, asked if they'd ever heard of a citizen's arrest. Malanzky said they had their rights.

I recited the Miranda warning.

They insisted that they wanted their lawyers, and I told them that they could call them now and have them meet us at the Hall of Justice.

Helpless looks; they probably didn't know any lawyers.

We took them downtown.

1:10 p.m.
A long, exhausting passage of time. Hy and I had given statements to SFPD detectives and FBI agents under the harsh neon lights of an interrogation room at 850 Bryant Street — a monolithic, forbidding stone building.

At first they were rough on me, especially the feds: why had I been hiding since the warrants went out on me?

I hadn't been hiding, I asserted. I'd simply been taking a few mental health days, not answering my phones or doorbell or going out. My office manager had kept me apprised of what was happening at the agency — events that had made me reluctant to resurface.

Their expressions said they'd believe that when giraffes could fly — another of Ma's malapropisms. Finally one of the SFPD inspectors spoke in a conciliatory tone. "None of us really believed you'd tried to drown Hoffman in the Bay. The APB was our way of getting hold of you so we could find out what really happened."

"A simple appointment at my office would've worked better."

They all ignored my remark. Then one of the feds asked if my husband was Hy Ripinsky, who was currently being interrogated in another room. One and the same, I replied. Added that if this was going the way I thought it was, I wanted my attorney, Glenn Solomon, present.

The SFPD detectives exchanged glances. They'd tangled with Glenn many times before.

"You're free to call Solomon," one finally said.

I really didn't want Glenn there any more

than they did. Apparently they had no knowledge of Jay Givens, so I didn't want to bring Glenn into this until I could talk with him privately.

"You know," I said, "if you'd questioned me politely and respectfully, as I would a member of an allied profession, I wouldn't be insisting on bringing in a high-powered and frequently obstructive attorney."

Startled expressions.

"Why don't we start over?" I added. "You've got a lot of information from my own staff, as well as what you've found out on your own. I'd like to hear your version."

They laid their case out for me, linking Van Hoffman and the Night Searchers. They'd arrested Hoffman, but he wasn't talking. "We'll break him down, though. It's only a matter of time and pressure," one of the feds said.

What kind of pressure? I wondered. Waterboarding?

When they finished, telling me little that I didn't already know, they left me alone for a few minutes, during which I laid my head on my arms on the metal table like a kindergartener. Then an inspector — Wesley Moore, I thought his name was — returned and said, "Come with me, Ms. McCone. All the Night Searchers have lawyered up, but the attorney for the one who calls himself Malanzky has advised his client to cooperate with us."

He took me to another room with one-way glass and indicated I should watch through it. Malanzky sat at the table next to a poorly dressed man who evidently was a public defender, and two uniformed cops flanked them. Plainclothes inspectors, Brenda Barcy and Frank Collins, sat across the table.

Brenda Barcy said to the lawyer, "You realize this doesn't imply a plea bargain will be offered? That's up to the district attorney."

"Yes, we understand. My client's actions have weighed heavily on his mind recently. He's chosen to unburden himself."

"Just so you're aware." She nodded to Malanzky. "Your turn, sir."

After a moment, he began in a quavering voice. "We were just this bunch of people, you couldn't even call us friends. I mean, we didn't even know each other's real names. All we did was play pranks. For fun."

"Why?" Frank Collins asked.

"Why? 'Cause that was what we did."

"People paid you to perform these 'pranks,' right?"

". . . Sometimes."

"Who?"

"I dunno."

Barcy stood up, leaned across the table toward him. *"Who?"*

". . . Well, there was this one guy, wanted to play a joke on his old lady on their wedding anniversary. She didn't much like it."

"His name?"

"Uh . . . uh . . . dunno, but he lives on Russian Hill."

"Go on," she said.

"There was a woman in Pacific Heights. Wanted us to scare the hell out of her husband for some reason, pretend we were going to beat him up."

"Just pretend?"

"That's all. He came at us with a rifle and we took off."

"His name?"

"I don't remember. I'm no good with names."

"What about Van Hoffman?" Barcy asked.

"I dunno anything about him."

"How much did your so-called clients pay you?"

"Don't know that either. The Griz handled all our finances."

"Was the Griz in control of everything?"

"Well, there was Supercom."

"Who's that?"

"I dunno. The Griz was pretty close-mouthed with information about him. I kinda suspected he didn't exist. You know, like he was somebody to lay the blame on if anything went wrong."

"So you think Grizeldy was the mastermind of the whole scheme?"

He frowned. "I dunno. Griz didn't strike me as too smart."

"Maybe she had help."

"From who?"

Indeed from whom? As Malanzky hesitated, my mind ranged through the list of Grizeldy's associates. None of them seemed particularly bright.

Collins asked, "What about a man named Jay Givens? His wife —"

A flush spread slowly up Malanzky's throat to his face, and he turned to his lawyer. ". . . I think I'm not gonna talk any more. That's my right, isn't it?"

"Absolutely."

The detectives looked at each other and shrugged. End of interview with a perp. The world according to Miranda.

9:02 p.m.

I banged on the door of Glenn Solomon's Italianate house in St. Francis Wood — an exclusive neighborhood west of Twin Peaks where he and Bette had moved last year. There was no response, so I banged again. A light was on in Glenn's library on the lower story. I watched as more lights flashed in progression to the entry.

Glenn, clad in a maroon terry cloth bathrobe, peered out at me. "My friend, what are you doing here at this ungodly hour?"

I pushed past him. "There's nothing ungodly about this hour."

"There is if you're dressed for bed and listening to Mendelssohn."

"Tough. I'm sick and tired of you ducking my calls. Why have you been hiding from me?"

He sighed heavily. "Because I can't lie to you. I never could. And client confiden—"

"If I hear that word one more time, I'm going to run amok."

Glenn took my elbow and propelled me down the hall to his library. It was a very masculine room, probably designed by Bette. Music filtered softly through speakers mounted on one wall.

"Drink?" he asked.

I shook my head. "Information."

"About?"

"The Givenses."

". . . All right." He sat down in an easy chair, but I remained standing.

"You haven't been up-front with me," I said. "Not at all. Why?"

"I was afraid I might've prejudiced your investigation."

"How?"

"With my suspicions about them."

"What suspicions?"

"Nothing specific. Just that hinky feeling I mentioned."

"Did it ever occur to you to examine that 'hinky feeling'?"

"It didn't seem important. I knew you'd get to the bottom of it."

"And it never occurred to you that you might be putting me in danger because I didn't know all the nuances of the case?"

"If I had, I would have —"

"I am so sick of these excuses! Lawyers lying and covering up for their clients —"

"Wait till you're in trouble and need one. You'll thank me then."

"You pompous son of a bitch!"

Glenn drew back as if I'd slapped him. I'd never before called him names or spoken to him in such a tone.

I pressed on. "For starters, in the files you let me see you noted that an HH had contacted you, and you referred him to Jay, who said he'd take care of it. What's an HH?"

"Oh, that." He rubbed his eyes. "The initials stand for *heir hunter.* Kind of a disreputable lot, but if their fees aren't too high, they occasionally help people out. They search for inheritances that haven't been claimed, contact the heir, and provide them with information on the bequests — for a fee."

"Steep fee?"

"Depends on the hunter and the amount of the bequest. In Camilla's case it was an aunt in New York whom she barely remembers."

"And the bequest was . . . ?"

"Privileged information. I shouldn't have told you what I already have."

"Stop stonewalling — we're not talking about some client's little secrets now. This is a damned serious matter. Did you report this information to her?"

"No, Jay said —"

"So she didn't know."

"He may have told her —"

"He didn't."

"Are you sure?"

"Positive."

"Well, he's always controlled their joint finances. But why would he hide it from her?"

"For greedy reasons. Ever since then he's

been siphoning a mixture of chemicals into her cigarette lighter that produces hallucinations. When she decided to quit smoking, he began having a group of weirdos he's associated with stage little horror shows in order to convince medical personnel that she's crazy."

"*What?* My God, Sharon, why?"

"So he can institutionalize her and control her inheritance."

Glenn was silent for several seconds. "Can you prove it? Because if you can't, the rules of confidentiality —"

"Jesus Christ!" I exclaimed. "I think the right to confidentiality has been trumped by gaslighting and attempted murder, don't you? If you insist, I can get a court order —"

Glenn grimaced, then rested his forehead on his hand. "That won't be necessary."

"How much is the bequest?" I asked.

He sat very still for several seconds, then raised his head. Even before he spoke his expression said he wasn't going to argue with me any longer.

"The estate hasn't been evaluated yet, but I would guess between fifteen and twenty million dollars."

"That much!"

"It's prime real estate in Brooklyn. An

area where development's going over the top. He said he would tell her about it and they would decide —"

Now he'd confirmed what I'd suspected Jay Givens had been up to. Camilla had no money of her own, but squandered his. She was eccentric, while his tastes ran to the conservative. Divorce was out of the question: under the state's community property laws, any and all assets would be equally split, and half of fifteen to twenty million wouldn't be enough for him. He wanted it all.

So what had he decided to do? Arrange some sort of fatal "accident"? No, the man didn't have it in him to do it himself, and hiring it out would be too dangerous. That left the mental institution and a conservatorship over her affairs.

And who better to spook her when she was in one of her drug-induced states than the Night Searchers, a group Jay occasionally associated with? As leverage, he'd gotten one of the Searchers to hide the plaque Grizeldy had contributed to their pool and had communicated that she could have it back once the group performed his bizarre charade. He'd also instructed the Searcher to hide it in her own freezer — an ironic touch that had Jay written all over it.

■ ■ ■ ■

SUNDAY, MARCH 18

■ ■ ■ ■

8:11 a.m.

I checked in with all my available operatives; most were out hunting for Jay Givens,
who had vanished from all his usual haunts.
None of them complained about sleeplessness or having to work on a Sunday; they
knew I'd give them plenty of paid free time
when the caseload lightened.

It took all the restraint I possessed to wait
to call Camilla Givens at a civilized hour.
But *is* there a civilized hour to tell someone
that her spouse is planning to have her committed to a mental institution? When I
finally did make the call, the operative at
the RI suite turned out to be Arthur Ames,
a longtime employee whom I knew well.

He said, "Ms. Givens didn't have a good
night."

"I expected that."

"I'll take the phone to her."

"Thank you, Arthur." Arthur, not Art; he

was a formal man, a published poet in his spare time.

Camilla came on the line, sounding shaky.

"I need to talk to you today," I said.

"I'll be here. I've seen enough of the outside world for a while."

"Know what you mean. How about if I come by around noon?"

"That'd be fine."

"One question for now: do you know anybody named Opal Carson?"

"Opal Carson." A pause. "I don't know her, but someone of that name left a message on our machine recently. I think she's Jay's physical therapist — he has a bad back, you know."

Right — a physical therapist who made her living as a chemist.

Chemist . . .

10:09 a.m.

I'd taken Derek off the Opal Carson stakeout the day before, but now I called and asked him to meet me across from her apartment building on Balboa Street, where I found him browsing through the bins of fruit and vegetables outside a corner grocery.

He must've sensed my presence beside him, because he said, "Do you know that if

338

you eat these every day you'll live ten years longer?"

He indicated something that looked like a cross between a rutabaga and a turnip. Uglier than both too. The sign below it said "mulzini."

"I'd rather die young. Well, middle-aged, anyway."

"Me too."

"So what's happening over there?" I motioned at Opal Carson's apartment house.

"Lots of people coming and going. Not our Mr. Givens, though."

"These people —"

"They don't look like druggies, but they are — the genteel variety."

"Meaning?"

"Well dressed, expensive cars. Buying stuff like uppers or downers. Maybe performance enhancers, steroids. I just saw the agent of a prominent local athlete come and go. The woman's running a regular pharmacy over there."

"Any chance of going in undercover?"

"I can try." He took out his wallet and showed me a business card that identified him as a physical trainer. "After all, my clients need to build up their abs and pecs."

I smiled as I watched him cross the street;

I myself had amassed a large collection of cards of people in various professions, and had found that there's nothing like a crisp rectangular piece of cardboard to gain entry to all sorts of places. Derek was admitted to the apartment after a bit of initial questioning. Then I walked a block to a café where we'd agreed to meet, ordered coffee, and waited.

11:17 a.m.
Derek sat down in the chair next to mine. "Easy," he said.

"Oh yeah?"

He handed me a bottle with a Safeway pharmacy label attached. The label claimed the blue pills inside were sleep aids. "She says they're 'safe steroids.' "

"I'll send them to Richman Labs for analysis. What's she like?"

"The term 'witchy' applies. Maybe it's an act she puts on for her customers — she's only open on Sundays, you know. But black hair streaked with silver, purple lipstick and nail polish, multiple piercings and tattoos, and clothes that show everything but her twat — that's witchy."

"I'd've thought you'd enjoy clothes like that."

"Mostly what they did was show more tattoos. You know I'm sorry I ever had this done." He touched the snake tat around his neck.

"Why do you suppose somebody like Jay Givens would be attracted to her?"

"For the drugs, of course. And she's so different from the norm. There's something about her that's so earthy, so elemental, so evil . . . was I just repetitive?"

"It's called 'alliterative' when applied to poetry."

"Poetry? First time in my life. You see what a woman like that can do to a man?"

12:01 p.m.

Camilla greeted me warmly and seated me on the couch while the RI man went to the kitchen for coffee.

"I suppose you're wondering where I went last night?" she asked.

"I know where you went. Home to see your husband."

"Yes."

"Why?"

"To tell him I want a divorce. I can't stand to be with him any more."

"What did he say?"

"He wasn't there. So I walked around for a while — didn't feel like going inside even though I have a key — and when he still wasn't home, I came back here."

"Jay's claiming you went inside and trashed the condo in a rage."

Her dark-blue-ringed eyes grew wide. "I *what*?"

"Since it was only your possessions that were damaged, I think we can assume he did it."

"Why would he?"

"He seems bent on proving that you're mentally unstable. He's responsible for what's been happening to you, all the things you believe you witnessed. They weren't real, Camilla."

"They . . . they weren't?"

"No: all the hallucinations, the bizarre experiences. Jay was infusing your cigarette lighter — the gold Dunhill — with a mixture of butane and other chemicals that cause such problems. I had the residue analyzed."

"Where did you get the lighter?"

"I found it where you must've dropped it in the vacant lot where you believed you saw babies being sacrificed. Those gatherings were staged especially for you by a group called the Night Searchers that Jay's been a part of."

"This is a lot to take in." She put her hand to her forehead. "Why would Jay want to make me think I'm crazy? If it's another woman — and there have been plenty — why didn't he just divorce me?"

"Think back to when these incidents started. Did anything significant change in your lives around then?"

A long pause. "No, not that I remember."

"All right, then. What matters most to Jay?"

"Money and status. But mainly money."

"Were there any changes in your financial state around that time?"

". . . No. I think he may have lost money in the stock market, but not enough to worry about. Jay believes the market always corrects itself."

Well, it usually does, but often it's a long, slow process. And Jay was clearly not a patient man.

I said, "I think there was a definite change for the better in your financial situation, but only Jay knows about it." Then I proceeded to tell her what I'd found out from Glenn.

12:36 p.m.

"Fifteen to twenty *million* dollars? I don't believe it!"

"Believe it — it's all yours." I watched Camilla as the news began to sink in.

"This great-aunt who left me this . . . this fortune," she finally said. "I didn't even

343

know about her."

"Apparently the last time she saw you was when you were a baby."

"Who was she?"

I took out the fact sheet Glenn had given me. "Emily Rosenthal. Your maternal grandmother's sister. She never married or had children, but she sure knew how to pick her real estate."

"But how did she know where to find me?"

"She didn't, so she asked her attorney that upon her death, he should take the usual steps."

"What steps?"

"Generally, announcements in prominent newspapers across the country, requesting information about an individual's whereabouts. That's probably where this heir hunter learned of the bequest. Sometimes the attorneys hire them, but not in your case."

"So this guy located Jay and me, but talked to Jay first. Why would he do that?"

"Plain old sexism, I'd guess. Or maybe he tried to reach you but couldn't."

"And Jay decided he wanted my inheritance all for himself." She took a cigarette from a silver box on the end table, looked around for matches, then replaced it in the box.

"I'd like my lighter back," she said after a moment. "I've mostly quit smoking, but that lighter belonged to my father, and I'm sentimental."

"You'll get it back after the trial."

She pushed her fingers through her hair. "There *will* be a trial, then?"

"Probably several. There's Jay, the Night Searchers, and there may be others who were involved."

"And all because some money I didn't know existed was willed to me by a great-aunt I don't remember."

"You're a wealthy woman now, Camilla. First thing you should do is divorce Jay."

"And it will be. You know . . . I first thought of ending the marriage last fall. But I changed my mind because we had such a nice Christmas — it made me believe in us again." Tears were welling in her eyes.

"Well," I said, "if I were you, I'd contact a lawyer immediately. Glenn can recommend someone good."

She nodded. "But for now — Jay doesn't know where I am, does he?"

"No."

"Have you told the police yet what he's done to me?"

"I thought you might want to do that, make the formal complaint. We'll all be available to back you up."

For a moment she sagged, then sat up straighter. "I'll do it. I *can* do it."

"But not just yet," I told her. "Let me have my turn at him first."

"Fine with me. The first time we met you, Jay said he didn't like or trust you."

"Well, maybe he was right."

4:35 p.m.

After a stop at the office, I joined Derek in his stakeout at the produce stand across the street from Opal Carson's apartment on Balboa.

"Business has been brisk over there," he told me. "I've never seen so many upscale people who want to exist in an altered state."

I moved to allow a woman to get at the bok choy. "We need to find a better observation point. You've been here too long."

"There's a phone booth around the corner. Nobody uses those any more."

But when you needed one — such as when your cell's battery died — you couldn't find one. I remembered the time I was at O'Hare Airport, en route to New York: the cell was dead, I needed to return a call, and I had to range for what seemed

346

like miles to locate a pathetic little kiosk blocked from view by candy and soda machines. We forget the fallibility of our technical devices until one of them quits on us. Not that landlines are any better: at Touchstone the wires are down in the strong coastal winds about as often as they're up.

"Okay," I said. "You head for the booth. I want to call Hy."

Hy answered his phone on the first ring. "How's it going?"

"Derek and I are waiting outside the Carson apartment house to see if Jay Givens shows up."

"Need company?"

"No. We're about to take shelter in a phone booth, and three won't fit."

"Don't touch his dick."

We both laughed: it was our favorite line from an outrageous old movie, *A Fish Called Wanda.*

"Ripinsky, when this case is over —"

"We're taking a long vacation."

"Hah."

"You don't believe me?"

"I believe you believe what you say."

"But . . . ?"

"I also believe in past experience."

"Well, we'll see."

We ended the call, and I went to the

phone booth. Derek took up so much room that I sat down on the pavement outside and acted like a homeless person.

7:50 p.m.
It was full dark, the lights having winked on all around us. I stood up, mostly because I was afraid of a passing patrol car rousting me, but also because my ass was cold and my muscles tight.

Derek moaned, "I could've had a date with one hot woman tonight."

"Call her."

"What?"

"I sense Givens has gone to ground. I'll stay here for a while, just in case he shows."

He took out his phone, and I resumed my sidewalk sitter's pose.

8:14 p.m.
The fog was in and the night felt chilly; the Avenues, especially in the area where Opal Carson lived, were wrapped in mist, only a few muted lights showing. Traffic was at a minimum. Every half an hour or so I'd get up from my slumped position by the phone booth and walk around to warm myself, keeping my eyes on the building across from the now-closed produce stand. I was about to give it up as a lost cause. One more stroll

up and down the block, I promised myself, then home.

I was on Sixteenth, almost to the intersection with Balboa, when a dark figure appeared from between a couple of Dumpsters that were pulled in close to the curb. I backed up, prepared for flight, but strong hands grabbed my shoulders and pushed me back into the alley behind the building that housed the produce stand. My feet banged into wooden crates and I smelled rotted fruit and vegetables. I slipped on a slick place, an arm encircled my neck and pulled me upright.

Then I heard a snicking sound — the safety being taken off an automatic. The gun's muzzle jammed into the bone behind my right ear.

"Don't try to struggle, Sharon. I'll shoot you right here if you do." The voice, tense and nervous, belonged to Jay Givens.

I stood still, cursing myself for walking into an ambush like a damned amateur. I should've anticipated the possibility that Givens had already arrived, by a different route, and set himself up where he could watch and wait for an opportunity like this.

"You don't want to shoot me, Jay."

"The hell I don't. You've spoiled everything, you and Camilla."

"Yes, and we're not the only ones who know the truth. You can't get away with killing me."

"I can try."

"Use your head, Jay. You're not stupid — why risk adding a murder charge to the other ones against you?"

"Shut up. Just shut up!" He jabbed my ear with the gun muzzle. "My car's up the street. We're going for a ride."

"Where?"

"Never mind where. Let's go. No, wait. You armed?"

Even though I wasn't, I said, "Yes."

"Where's your weapon?"

"Coat pocket."

"Take it out with your thumb and forefinger and drop it."

"No."

"Damn you, do what I tell you!"

"You don't drop guns on pavement," I said. "They're liable to go off accidentally when they hit."

". . . All right, then. Take it out and lay it down. Slow and careful."

I put my hand in my coat pocket, bending my knees as if to lower myself into a squatting position. He followed suit, leaning against me slightly so that he had to be a little off balance. I lunged upward, swiveling my body, knocked the gun aside with my left arm, and slammed my right fist into his face.

The suddenness of the move, the last thing he expected from a woman, caught him completely unaware. He staggered backward, reflexively squeezing the automatic's trigger, and the gun went off with a hollow roar. The slug missed me by several feet, thudding into the side of one of the Dumpsters. The recoil threw Givens further off balance, giving me a chance to wrap my fingers around the hot barrel and tear the weapon loose from his grasp. But I couldn't hold on to it. I heard it fall clattering to the pavement.

He tried to head-butt me, but I side-stepped in time, caught hold of his coat in both hands, and brought my knee up into his groin. Direct hit. His shriek of pain told me so, gave me more satisfaction than it probably should have. He bent over double, clutching his wounded privates, and stumbled around banging into the Dumpsters and crates.

Even as dark as it was, I managed to find the gun without having to crawl on all fours looking for it. Large-caliber weapon, a .45. More firepower than a man like Givens knew how to use in close quarters or I'd probably have been dead or disabled instead of standing there unhurt.

Reaction set in then. One of those moments when your knees have a jellied feel and your mind goes into overdrive, images passing so quickly you can barely identify them. I took several deep breaths to steady myself and clear my head. I didn't have anything more to fear from Givens; he'd slumped to one knee, still clutching himself.

After a few seconds he looked up at me. I couldn't see his eyes, but they must have been as sick as his voice sounded. "You bitch," he whimpered, "you broke my balls."

"Call me a bitch again and I'll do more than that."

The gunshot had attracted attention. A couple of people came running up, and I yelled to them to call 911. One of them obeyed, while the other stayed to gawk at a safe distance.

I waited to be relieved of my moaning prisoner.

■ ■ ■ ■

MONDAY, MARCH 19

■ ■ ■ ■

1:10 a.m.

"So that's that," I said to Hy as we snuggled under a faux fur throw in front of the kiva-style fireplace in our living room. "All the damn perps in these two crazy cases are in custody."

"Right. Van Hoffman finally confessed to fraud, embezzlement, and hiring the Searchers to harass you. The cops and feds didn't even have to lean on him too much. He talked and talked. I think now they wish he'd *stop* talking."

"So what was his plan?" I asked.

"Originally, to fake his kidnapping, collect the ransom, and run off to South America with his girlfriend. Of course, the whole scenario was doomed from the start. He was foolish enough to think that his wife would fall for a ransom demand that was nearly the exact amount of their savings — and that she cared enough about him to pay it.

When she refused, he came up with another fake plan, again with the help of the Night Searchers — pretending two of them were his kidnappers throwing him into the Bay. He counted on those two as witnesses; what he didn't expect was two genuine witnesses with a night scope and infrared camera. Or one who could swim well."

"And then he told that ridiculous story about me trying to drown him."

"That nobody believed, but sent you into panic mode."

"Don't remind me." I sighed. "But what damn fools some men can be."

Hy grinned. "Especially the ones looking to run away from home."

"That's what kids do."

"Let's face it: we're not dealing with an adult personality here."

"You can say that again. So are all the other details on the Night Searchers cases wrapped up?"

"More or less. The freelance enforcer who uses Bay Rum cologne — the reason you and the old guy on the waterfront smelled lime on him — admitted he'd been hired by a friend of Jay Givens, but has conveniently forgotten his name. The guy you chased from the Municipal Pier before the Griz's car crapped out on you was a Night Searchers hanger-on who's since vanished. As for the Kenyons, they'll probably bicker over that vacant lot until one of them dies or gives in and builds something there."

"Oh," I said, "right. I forgot to tell you: they got into a brawl last night at a restaurant in Rome. Spaghetti draped over their ears, lasagna smeared on their faces, lots of good Chianti wasted."

"How did you find that out?"

"Google News."

"Of course."

I reached for my wine — a wonderful Alexander Valley zin that we'd been saving for a special occasion. "One question," I said. "What did the so-called 'fanatics' in the Global Policy Forum plan? Did they have an agenda?"

"Not that any of the people from Washington who've been swarming all over here can figure. They think, and I agree, that was just a smoke screen for Hoffman's scenario for escaping his real life."

"God, a lot of marriages are fucked up, but the ones in this case are real cautionary tales."

Hy snuggled closer to me, took a sip of my wine. "What about our marriage?"

I smiled. "We have each other — although it's a wonder, after all the tough times we've gone through. We have our health, our friends and relatives and cats. We have our homes. And we also have a business to run."

"A business — singular?"

I looked into his eyes. They were hopeful, yearning.

"A business — singular."

Now his eyes sparkled, and a grin spread over his face.

"We may squabble over things from time to time," I said, "but we do work well together. What should we call our new company?"

"Ripinsky and McCone International?"

"Wrong order. McCone and Ripinsky."

"Why?"

"Alphabetical."

"But my name —"

"Is only prominent on the international front. Mine is well known in the Western states. And I'm not sure about the 'International.' "

"But RI has offices in thirty-seven countries."

"A lot of which are nothing more than mail drops."

"But —"

"Stop squabbling, Ripinsky. We'll work out the details later, to our mutual satisfaction. *Casablanca*'s on the late late show in five minutes, and I want popcorn to go with it."

He sighed and stood up. "I'll do the popping, you melt the butter."

ABOUT THE AUTHOR

Marcia Muller has written many novels and short stories. Her novel *Wolf in the Shadows* won the Anthony Boucher Award. The recipient of the Private Eye Writers of America's Lifetime Achievement Award and the Mystery Writers of America Grand Master Award—their highest accolade—she lives in northern California with her husband, mystery writer Bill Pronzini.

The employees of Thorndike Press hope you have enjoyed this Large Print book. All our Thorndike, Wheeler, and Kennebec Large Print titles are designed for easy reading, and all our books are made to last. Other Thorndike Press Large Print books are available at your library, through selected bookstores, or directly from us.

For information about titles, please call:
(800) 223-1244

or visit our Web site at:
http://gale.cengage.com/thorndike

To share your comments, please write:
Publisher
Thorndike Press
10 Water St., Suite 310
Waterville, ME 04901

BOOK "MARKS"

If you wish to keep a record that you have read this book, you may use this space to mark a private code. Please do not mark the book in any other way.
